THE STARSHIP FROM SIRIUS

By
ROG PHILLIPS

I0616942

ARMCHAIR FICTION
PO Box 4369, Medford, Oregon 97501-0168

*For more information about Armchair Books and products, visit our
website at…*

www.armchairfiction.com

Or email us at…

armchairfiction@yahoo.com

HOSTILE VISITORS FROM THE STARS?

In the Martian year 3947 a strange ship was discovered approaching from space, getting ready to land—visitors from the stars! Would they be hostile? No one knew. There was no contact, no response, and its very presence seemed distinctly sinister to the overwrought imaginations of the people of Mars. When the ship finally landed, Dr. Irwin Crabtree and his two military escorts entered the ship's open hatch and made a shocking discovery: Descendants of star voyagers that had left Earth many centuries before! They soon found themselves hurtling through space in an unexpected journey that nothing could have prepared them for.

Join master science fiction storyteller Rog Phillips for a fascinating yet grim look at the Earth of the future in his brilliant sequel to "So Shall Ye Reap."

FOR A COMPLETE SECOND NOVEL, TURN TO PAGE 135

CAST OF CHARACTERS

LES TURNER
This famed reporter had the grim duty of reporting the details of the construction of Mankind's last hope—a colossal spaceship.

JACK JANES
He volunteered to make outer space repairs to his crippled spacecraft—unfortunately it would probably cost him his life!

IRWIN CRABTREE
Entering a mysterious spaceship with an armed guard was one thing, but being thrown out into space was not what he expected.

ARTURO
Helping his friend might mean certain death, but for a chance to finally see Earth, he'd risk it!

DELLA
This beauty wasn't afraid to battle a few bugs in order to save her people—and the man she loved.

STELLA
Faced with a horrific situation, she could only hope she was strong enough for the terrifying fight that lay ahead.

PART ONE

THE silver sphere had been circling the planet for several days, going in the opposite direction to the two moons. It had slowed rapidly until now its speed was no more than half what it should be to stay in its orbit: yet it did not plunge Marsward, but remained a uniform two thousand miles away from the surface.

Irwin Crabtree—Dr. Crabtree to his fellows, turned his giant telescope on it the moment it appeared above the horizon and (the precise clockwork kept the sphere in the exact center of the eyepiece until it dropped beneath the horizon once again.)

Obviously, since the sphere violated the proven mathematics of astronomy, it must be a space ship. Equally obviously, it must be preparing to land—slowing its forward speed, holding itself away from the atmosphere until its speed had been reduced to practically nothing.

These things must be so, even though there was neither tell-tale rocket blast nor other visible indication of the thrust forces being used to effect these ends.

The four hundred inch Orno Observatory telescope brought the ship so close that parts of the sphere could be studied. The spectroscope showed the material of the sphere to be a metallic alloy unknown to science in the year 3947. The eyepiece showed structural regularities such as the rectangular bands about the circumference of the ship.

The two self-luminous areas at what must be the poles of the sphere were unexplainable high temperature areas. They shifted, pointing now forward and to the stern in the line of orbit, now shifting so that one disappeared and the other pointed toward the surface of Mars. When that happened there were magnetic storms on Mars. Not violent, but detectable with nothing more than a compass. The magnetic storms were not accompanied by electric display as those from the sun were.

The mass of the sphere could not be determined. In size, however, it was exactly three thousand feet in diameter.

The sphere had first been sighted two years before. Then it had been just a bright speck of no appreciable size, five degrees ten minutes and twenty-seven seconds under, and fifteen seconds to the west of Sirius.

The four hundred inch telescope had made possible spectroscopic analysis of its light, and the results had created a sensation overnight. Since then the progress of the "star" had been closely observed. It was not until it passed the orbit of Pluto, however, that it had been brought within range of magnification so that its shape could be determined.

Visitors from the stars! Would they be hostile? No one knew. Both Mars and Venus diverted production to the building of a ring of huge cyclotronic defense batteries about their respective planets.

When the sphere settled in an orbit about Mars—the entire power output of the planet went into the huge cyclotrons, and pale beams of incredible power contacted and went into the mystery ship.

The only visible effect had been a measured increase in temperature of the poles of the ship. After ten hours of this pouring of destructive power into the vessel the Martian Government had ordered the cyclotrons shut off pending further deliberation.

No answering message had come from the sphere to the continuous barrage of beamed broadcasts directed at it. So far, it might as well be a robot-controlled ship with no life on board.

This theory became popular and was elaborated upon, until the general public became convinced that the crew of the ship must be in suspended animation. Certainly no creature similar to man could cross the void from a distant star in one life span unless he found some way of suspending animation and stalling off old age.

One writer advanced the theory that perhaps this ship might contain the answer to the mystery of the solar system.

ON two planets, and two only, in all the solar system was there Intelligent life; Mars and Venus. Since before the earliest written records these two races had risen from savagery to civilization, arriving at the same time independently. Both had discovered radio in the same generation and developed it rapidly to the point where they soon were able to contact each other across space.

Then had come the BIG surprise. Their languages had the same root forms. The two supposedly independently evolved races were identical.

As the two planets became rapidly acquainted they received a third great surprise. Each numbered its years according to a custom handed down from pre-history, whose origin was unknown. Only, on Mars it was the year 2748, and on Venus it was the year 4182.

The brilliant Martian mathematician, Hugo Branding, had mixed these up with the length of the Martian and Venusian years and come out with a mystical number, 1954. What this number meant, no one knew. But it pointed to the possibility that 794 Mars years before, or 2,228 Venus years before, whichever way you looked at it, had been the year 1954 on BOTH planets.

That year was lost to the memories of both planets although the mythology of those times, handed down from generation to generation, was similar on both, and spoke of a common origin on some unknown third planet, or at the very least a common origin on one or the other of the two inhabitable planets.

1954 became a mystical number associated with religion. Prophecies were based on manipulation of this magic number—and the prophecies invariably failed.

Then had come rocket flight, possible from Mars but not from Venus. The first Martians had landed on Venus barely alive. It was then proven that the two races separated by worlds were the same race, and offspring of the men who had lived long enough to get to Venus were still flourishing. They were the "four hundred" of Venus, living on pension and receiving special training each generation.

A second group of volunteers, now knowing their adventure would be suicide, had made it to the Earth, that stormy, radioactive planet, and lived long enough to transmit millions of television images to Venus which was then in the most favorable position for radio communication. They had placed books and newspapers under the television eyes and turned their pages while cameras recorded their contents on far off Venus. Then they had died.

The great immediate discovery from this trip had been that all dated material on the Earth had had the years numbered. The magical 1954 appeared on much of the material, and also the three succeeding numbers, but nothing with a year number greater than 1957 had been transmitted.

The reason for this might be one of many. It could be assumed that the suicide explorers had not had time to finish, and that material of later dates had been ready for transmission when they died from cosmic ray burns. It could also be postulated that the civilization on the Earth had ceased to exist after 1957.

Regardless of that, it seemed conclusive that the mystery of 1954 had been cleared up. The Earth was the parent planet, and in that historic year colonizers had landed on both Mars and Venus. This theory accounted for everything except how and why the parent race had died so suddenly, and why no more colonizers had come.

SPACE travel had been abandoned after this final success. It had been demonstrated that the deadly rays of interplanetary space were invariably fatal. There was no longer a strong reason for men to sacrifice their lives in such voyages. Television brought both inhabited planets together socially and culturally so that a man on Mars made his friends on Venus and vice versa. And thus matters had stood.

The material from the Earth had been catalogued and studied, and much of it had been transmitted to Mars. Many scientific advances had been made from study of that material. The languages of both planets had been successfully traced in their roots to that of Earth.

But there were no traces of successful interplanetary flight among those records, nor any hint concerning the flight that MUST have been made, that left the first ancestors of the present races on Mars and Venus.

The cataloguing had been according to a subject system, so that in the analyzer all the cards on one subject would be sorted out and the material obtained at once. When this work was finally completed the G-22 V-7 run was blank, indicating no items about colonizing or even landing on Mars and Venus.

That did not mean there absolutely wasn't any mention of such voyages. It merely meant that if there was such mention it had been misclassified by the cataloguers due to its vagueness or apparent meaning. Mastery of the ancient language was growing greater each year, and continual revision of the master catalogue went on all the time.

AND now, in the Martian year 3947 a strange ship was hovering out in space, getting ready to land. A ship that was a perfect sphere of polished metal three thousand feet in diameter, with no rocket ports of any sort. A ship that had entered the solar system from the direction of Sirius.

Perhaps in it, too, the living had been long ago blasted by space rays, just as the space pioneers from Mars had been. Perhaps it had been traveling for millions of years under robot control until finally it had neared a sizable planet and the robot pilot had set into motion the routine of landing.

But such a theory was self-contradictory because it implied long development of the technique of space flight, and consequently safeguards against space rays. Certainly the ship was immune to the greatest destructive power that the planet could unleash against it. It had also undoubtedly repulsed collisions with asteroids without receiving a scratch that could show in even the four hundred inch Orno Observatory telescope at a distance of a few hundred miles, and at that distance even a scratch would show unmistakably.

The population was very jittery. It had good cause to be. Visible every day was a huge, silent orb, hanging like a threat over all. It hinted at science far beyond anything even the wildest dreamers could imagine, and at a race of Beings from some other part of the universe who KNEW that science. Its very silence, coupled with its mysterious power of movement, seemed nothing but sinister to the overwrought imaginations of the people of both Mars and Venus.

There was little question that if the ship were inimical it would have to be dealt with by Venus as soon as it finished with Mars. The only advantage the Venusians would have would be a few days in which they knew exactly what they could expect, if that could be called an advantage in a fight against superscience.

Therefore Irwin Crabtree sat in the saddle before the eyepiece of the giant telescope and watched the passage of the sphere across the heavens, determining the elements of its trajectory and relating these elements to the ones derived the day before and the day before that.

The figures checked as he knew they would. The observatory mathematicians had taken the initial trajectory elements of the mysterious ship and from them built up an ideal landing schedule. Day after day the strange ship slowed in accordance with this ideal, proving the intention to land and also the fact that either a living crew or a perfect machine was controlling that sphere.

Today's calculations moved the certainty of the answer three places deeper into the decimal number.

Now Irwin asked the question uppermost in the minds of the people of Mars. He didn't ask it as a question, but stated it as a problem, speaking through the intercom to the mathematicians in their office in the lower part of the observatory.

"DETERMINE," he said, "The latitude and longitude of the point of landing."

At once a voice spoke from the intercom.

"We already have, doctor," it said. "Since you didn't request it we did not report it, but we have carried the problem out to that point each time to satisfy our own curiosity."

"Then report," Irwin Crabtree said tonelessly, but there was a smile lurking at the corners of his mouth which did not carry into his professional voice.

"We've assumed that a ship of that size would contact the stratosphere directly over the point of landing so as not to travel any further than necessary through the atmosphere. We base that assumption on economy of power consumption and the tremendous size of the ship. Each day the probable area of landing has narrowed down. Now we are certain that the ship intends to land in the valley five miles north of here. Its objective is Orno itself!"

"I rather suspected that all along," Irwin said slowly. "That speaks very well of their motives. They must know an observatory when they see one."

Irwin shut off the intercom. His eyes brooded on the sphere.

For perhaps twenty minutes he remained motionless— almost without breathing. Then reluctantly his hand reached to the instrument board and his finger flicked a switch marked "Venus Central."

Instantly a feminine voice spoke. "We are ready, sir. You have top priority for any message."

"Take a letter," Irwin answered. "It's to Dr. J.R. Boniface, Custodian of the Archives. Dear Dr. Boniface."

"Yes," the feminine voice answered.

"I have reason to suspect the existence of item A437 C665. Please determine if I am right at once and if so transmit item complete without delay."

The operator repeated the message. He O.K.'d it and flicked the switch to the off position.

The sphere disappeared behind the horizon on its circuit around the other side of Mars.

Irwin drummed his fingers slowly on the table of the instrument board, a faraway look in his eyes. After a few moments he climbed out of the saddle and descended to the floor of the observatory room.

His footsteps were slow and uncertain as he crossed the tile floor to the exit. He was getting old. Over fifty Martian years now.

In the hallway outside he took the elevator to a lower floor. When it stopped he slid back the door and crossed the hall to a door marked Dr. I. S. Crabtree, Director.

Almost immediately a messenger boy entered and handed him a packet of Photostats. The heading on them was ITEM: Section A437 C665, Heading: Space Ship Nearing

Completion, Everett, Wash. AP, March 5, 1953, and then a letter:

CUSTODIAN OF THE ARCHIVES
663 427 57th Lane North
53rd sublevel, the Hub
Feb. 14, 3947

VENUS

Dr. I. S. Crabtree
University of Orno
Orno, Mars

Dear Dr. Crabtree:

As per request in yours of February 14, 3947, am sending under separate cover the item on the last projected space flight, derived from the morgue of one of the newspapers of that time and preserved here in our archives.

The item is a series of articles written by a reporter of that era, and is in our opinion a most comprehensive account of the event from every standpoint. I trust this will fulfill your requirements.

Yours truly,
Dr. J. R. Boniface

ITEM: Section A437 665

Heading:
Space Ship Nearing Completion
Everett, Washington AP
March 5, 1953

Les Turner.

(Ed. introduction) This is the first of a series of articles written especially for the readers of this paper by Les Turner, noted news commentator, on the space ship now under construction on the tide flats at Everett, Washington. As you know, this is perhaps the most vital subject under discussion in the world today. The complete failure of all attempts at space flight to date may culminate with a law prohibiting all attempts at space flight if this present attempt fails. In fact, it was only by the slimmest of margins that Congress allocated funds for the construction of this ship, and it is certain that the billions going into it will be the last ever spent unless this attempt succeeds or unless something new comes to light which will make success more probable.

This series of articles will continue from day to day, refreshing your mind on the history of space flight failures to date, and bringing you an eyewitness account of what is going on at Everett and in what ways the scientists there who are supervising construction think they have licked the bugs which have so far proven 100 percent fatal.

THE outer skin of the huge globe lying on the tide flats just south of Everett has been complete for several months. Believe me, it is an awe inspiring sight from the air. Exactly three thousand feet in diameter, the huge globe squats like a super dew drop at the edge of the glassy surface of the Sound as the plane from New York circles in the stratosphere for clearance to land at the local airport.

I am dictating this into my portable wire recorder as I look through the porthole of the plane, which is now dropping for a landing.

Three thousand feet in diameter! And it is costing ten million dollars for each one of those three thousand feet. Thirty billions of dollars.

The reasons for the huge size and terrific expense are obvious to those of you who have kept informed on space flight attempts. There have been fifteen attempts to leave the Earth in a ship up to now. The earlier ones were tried with rocket jets. Even when atomic power was used they failed for various reasons. The most important reason for failure was lack of material. Although the source of atomic power was more than plentiful it could only be used on the rocket principle, sending matter out through a tube and using the recoil to drive the ship.

This one is different. One of the things I intend to find out and bring you is the principle they intend to use on this ship. There are no rocket tubes in evidence and it is claimed that none is used. Just how the ship can move is a big mystery.

All of you are acquainted with the many unforeseen things that wrecked previous attempts to cross the void even the short distance to the moon.

You all know that Greg Jones died of cosmic ray burns within fifty minutes after he left the Earth's atmosphere. This had not been foreseen at the time.

It had been known that cosmic ray intensity was such that to cross to the moon and back would almost certainly condemn any man to death within a year after he returned. Jones had accepted this risk for the honor of being the first to do it. The cosmic ray counters on his ship showed several times the predicted concentration of these deadly rays, and one hour and fifteen minutes after Jones took off he collapsed at the microphone on his ship. That was in October, 1949. The ship never returned to Earth so far as we know.

I believe, and I intend to find out for certain whether it is so or not, that the huge size of this ship we are building here at Everett is to provide sufficient protection against the cosmic rays of space. The way I understand it there is a small center section where the crew can remain while the ship is in space and be relatively safe from cosmic rays. That may not be the truth. There are so many stories going around that it is hard for the average man to know which are true and which aren't. That is one of the main things I am going to do in this series of articles; ask the questions the common man is asking, and give you the answers the experts who are actually building this ship give me.

OUR plane is preparing to land now. There are many well known persons on it with me as passengers. The field is the famous McChord field, built during the last war for the army. It's located a few miles south of Everett, just west of Mukilteo on Puget Sound. It was at Mukilteo that the army had a munitions loading center during the war, and it was there that the atom bombs from the Hanford plant were loaded aboard ship to be carried to the south Pacific for the atom bomb attack on Japan.

This is a beautiful country around here. Out in the Sound is Whidbey Island. Across the sound is the Olympic Mountains, and to the east are the Cascades, so that all the year round there are snow-capped mountains on either side and to the northeast, while the weather remains that of almost perpetual summer.

The last time I was here at this airport was seven years ago in 1946. It wasn't until two years later that the field became a municipal airport serving Seattle and Everett, with its elaborate buildings and hangars to accommodate the huge stratoliners.

The city of Everett has grown rapidly in the past seven years. Then it was a small city whose principle industry was lumber and plywood. With the growing air freight traffic to Alaska and the Orient, and with McChord field already built—larger and better adapted to the changing conditions of transportation; and also the low cost of electric power supplied by Grand Coulee, industry has moved in and skyscrapers have gone up all over the place.

I rode into the city on an airport bus and rented a room at the new Old Sigh Hotel, named after the granddaddy of all mountains which can be seen on clear days across the waters of the Sound at the north end of the Olympic Range.

Now I am in a taxi headed for the space ship yard, my portable recorder safe in my room winding off the yards of wire, while I use my pocket radio and hand mike to dictate this article.

I remember this part of Everett from seven years ago. The old Everett Pacific Shipyard used to be here. During the last war it turned out dry-docks for the navy. That was one of the yards that made possible our huge mobile flotillas which could move around the world independent of any fixed bases.

It jutted southward into the Sound, built up by dumping gravel and clinkers onto the tide flats. Now this whole area has been built up in that way.

Ahead of me, rising far higher than the Empire State building, resting in a huge cradle whose supporting legs are each a thousand foot skyscraper a square block across, is the mirror smooth skin of the ship itself. It is gigantic beyond the imagination. Incredible! The slightest breeze produces a pressure of thousands of tons against it and causes it to vibrate.

The gate is just ahead now. The taxi driver is slowing down. The guards at the gate are soldiers.

Of course it wouldn't be showing, but rumor has it that this place is defended from all directions so that NOTHING could get at this huge ship. The reasons for that are obvious to everyone who reads the paper. Certain countries have protested the building of the ship because it might mean that it would make possible the establishment of V2 bases on the moon. Then the whole world would be vulnerable to rocket bombs.

WELL, I'm here at last. I have to wait at the gait until Lt. Dortmer comes. He's been assigned to take me around the place. The guard is a very nice fellow. What is your name? Corporal Richard Jeans? Would you like to say something to the public, Dick? Tell them how it feels to be around the greatest project in the history of the world. That's right, just speak like you're talking to me.

"It's quite an experience, sir. You get so that you feel the huge ship is alive. It has its moods that change with the weather. Some days it's restless and some days it's calm and contented. You get so that you find your own mood changes with it. It's so big that it dominates everything."

That's fine, Dick, You know, I think you are cut out to be bigger than a corporal. I doubt if anyone could have put in words quite so well what this huge shining sphere does to a person. At any rate, in a few days the whole country will know that you are a guard here, and read what you just said. Does that make you feel important?

"No, sir."

No? Well, that just shows you don't let a little success or publicity go to your head. You're a great guy, Dick. You're O.K.

"Here comes Lt. Dortmer, sir."

Lt. Dortmer is driving up in a jeep. This yard is as big as a city. It's surfaced with what they call black top out here—a mixture of asphalt and gravel.

Lt. Dortmer? I'm Les Turner of the Associated Press.

"Glad to meet you, Mr. Turner. I received my orders to place myself at your disposal. I understand that you are to have a completely free hand, ask any questions you wish, and go wherever you want, and I am to see that you get to do it."

That's right. Only call me Les. I don't know who you're talking about when you say Mr. Turner. When people do that I turn around to see who they're talking to.

"All right, Les. And you may as well call me Harvey, to make things equal."

By the way, Harvey, everything you say to me goes through my pocket radio to my recorder at the hotel, and will appear in newspapers all over the country.

"Did you say your recorder is at the hotel, Les?"

Yes, Why?

"Well, this is going to be a big disappointment to you, Les, but most of the places you will want to see are dense to radio. If you expect to record everything you had better send for your recorder."

Oh, oh!

"I have an idea. We can send a man for it. While he is getting it I can show you around some of the places that aren't dense. Just make out an order for him to get it and the hotel will let him into your room."

You're a smart boy, Harvey. I'll do that.

THAT should take care of that for you, sir. Now, I think perhaps you might like to visit our workshops and get some idea of how the prefabrication is done. Too bad you didn't visit us when the shell was being made. It's of a special stainless steel, a high temper spring steel, two inches thick, with all joints welded and X-ray inspected for flaws."

Only two inches thick? Why, I'd supposed it to be several feet thick!

"Oh, no. You see, this is a new type of steel that has the tensile strength of at least two feet of the old types. Actually it is even better than it sounds, because it has a give and elasticity to it. It will stop a meteor rock striking it at a speed of ten miles a second and throw it back into space.

"One of its best features is that its desirable qualities are not decreased by increase in temperature. This ship could drop in free fall from outside the Earth's atmosphere and hit the ground without harming any of the crew. The skin would heat up to white heat during the fall through the atmosphere, but would not melt nor collapse. When you see the elaborate shock absorber system built between the shell and the core you will understand why the ship could come to a dead stop from a speed of five hundred miles an hour without hurting any of the crew."

That sounds unbelievable! You said something about the core. What is that?

"The core is what you might call a ship within a ship. In size it's about the same as two ocean liners put together. It weighs a hundred thousand tons and is a sphere three hundred feet in diameter, full of compartments for the crew, the instruments, and the stores. It doesn't contain the power plant or the atomic fuel. Those are outside the innermost cosmic ray shield.

"The cosmic ray shields are fundamentally successive laminations of stainless steel and barium compounds and things I don't know about designed for maximum absorption with minimum weight and thickness."

"I'm wondering, Harvey. With all these layers of protection how in the devil are the people inside going to see where they're going?"

"Oh, that's simple, really, Les, You see, light is reflected by mirrors but cosmic rays aren't. So at every stage of shielding along the axis of the telescopes the shield is cut, with an under shield a little larger than the cut, and a mirror reflects the light over to one side and another reflects it down toward the core, so that it eventually gets to the eyes of the pilot without any chance of the penetrating cosmic rays following it."

Who invented that? It seems to me that must be one of the greatest single inventions of the century, Harvey.

"Oh, no, Les. It's just a simple thing that had to be solved in the details of planning. There are hundreds of much more ingenious devices in the ship. For example, the shock absorber system that absolutely prevents damage to life and limb is much more worthy of being classed as a great invention."

How does that work?

"The basic idea is fairly simple. It's found, except for the ratchet slide addition to it, in the spring and shock absorber set up on the wheels of an automobile. You'll get a better idea of how it works if I tell you what would take place if this ship were to strike the moon at a speed of five hundred miles per hour and bounce back like a tennis ball on a tennis court.

"We have the core suspended from the shell by a system of these shock absorbers. The shell itself is also a shock absorber. Now, when the outer skin comes to an abrupt halt at the moon's surface the core, or central sphere, still has thirteen hundred and fifty feet to go before it can't go any further. A uniform deceleration of slightly less than six and three tenths gravities brings the central sphere of the ship to a stop in just under four seconds with no bump. That's the best that can be done.

"You can see what it does. A sudden stopping force is applied that would spread a man out flat and crush every cell in his body. The shock absorber system spreads this instantaneous force out uniformly over a period of almost four seconds and makes it just tolerable in a deceleration suit. You know what they are. They were developed during the last war for dive bombers. Essentially they put pressure all over the body so that the blood won't pile up in one part and explode the blood vessels."

WHEW! You know, Harvey, I'm beginning to have a great deal of respect for the human mind when it can figure out things like that. What's this ratchet business?

"The ratchet slides freely while the deceleration is going on. When it stops, the ratchets hook the series of deceleration springs onto the shock absorbers, which let the springs return to their original positions more slowly. In this five hundred mile per hour head on collision I'm talking about the central core would return to the center in about five minutes and be ready for another bounce."

Hmm hmm. I get it.

"One more thing I should mention in connection with that, Les. Such a hit would wreck the power plant and telescope channels, as well as the cosmic ray shielding of the ship. It WOULD save the lives of the men, though, and they will have the equipment to repair the damage to the ship if they aren't fried by rays. In actual flight it is very improbable that such a catastrophe will ever occur. The ship will be able to land on the moon or any other body very slowly and without a bump.

"It is only in the event of power failure or unforeseen hits by meteors with masses of two hundred thousand tons or more that such a catastrophe could take place."

Much chance of that?

"Almost none. Meteors that size can be detected by radar in time to avoid. Power failure is something else. I would say that it is the one big question mark to this whole project. Don't ask me about that though. I've been instructed to let Dr. Janes explain that. He's the master mind of the power plant and drive setup. As you know, he invented it."

"Here we are at the entrance to the shops. They occupy the entire circle of buildings that form the cradle for the ship. You can see over to the left where the car tracks go in.

"At the beginning this project absorbed an average of twenty carloads of materials a day. Now it has dwindled to two or three a day.

"In here are the fabricating shops. They occupy strategic locations for a minimum moving of materials and finished parts. You can see from the thickness of the supporting columns here that about half the volume of each building is taken up with supporting columns to hold the ship in its cradle and prevent it from collapsing the buildings. If the ship didn't rest in this cradle the slightest breeze would send it rolling across the country and nothing could stop it."

It would? I thought the ship weighed at least a million tons!

"A million tons! Ha! It only weighs two hundred thousand tons loaded. With its volume it only weighs about twenty-five times as much as the same volume of air, and about a thirty-second as much as the same volume of water! Don't forget, Les, most of the volume of the ship is nothing but empty space inside that two inch thick shell of stainless steel."

"WATCH your eyes, Les. The arc from welding stainless steel is particularly dangerous to the eye. All the metal parts of the ship are of the same stainless steel. The main reason for that is that it is non-magnetic and will last forever.

"Of course, the transformer iron isn't stainless steel, and the conduits are of aluminum. Also there is practically every metal in existence in the various instruments aboard."

Those instruments! I want to find out about them. I've heard that some of them are distinctly new to science, and based on new basics that we didn't know about even a few years ago.

"That's right, Les. They were known as far back as 1947, but they weren't generally accepted as being proven. It was only after we ran into trouble trying to account for some of the things that happened on space ships after they left the atmosphere of the Earth that we were finally forced to consider them seriously. You'll have to be patient on that score you'll learn about them from the scientists—from Dr. Janes when he explains the drive setup, and from Dr. Tziek when he takes you through the control cabin later on."

WE walked past what are called slabs—flat cast iron grids six inches thick upon which the various metal small parts of the ship were being welded and formed. Men bare to the waist, their skins and clothing grimy with sweat and glistening in the reflected rays of the occasional welding arc worked on without looking up at us.

Overhead cranes whirred past us, swinging heavy metal sheets which swayed dangerously. The workers instinctively dodged them without seeming to look at them. The whine of metal saws at the far end of the shop made talking difficult.

The underside of the space ship could be seen in the distance, two blocks or more away. It seemed almost flat and perhaps it was since it probably flattened a little due to the flexibility of the shell.

It was at this point that a soldier caught up with us, carrying my portable recorder which I had been too lazy to bring with me. Evidently he had been ordered to follow us and carry it for me, because he made no motion to give it to me. I kept my tongue in my cheek and hoped that was the case, because I didn't like the prospect of carrying it myself all over the place.

"Most of the stuff is taken into the ship from underneath, Les. It goes up to the level where it is sent on elevators, then goes to the correct spot on cars. The interior of the ship is a honeycomb of skeleton structure that will have to be torn out when the ship is finished. You won't be able to see too much because of it.

"We'll stop at different levels though and go where we can see the huge shock springs. You'll be amazed at them. It's like looking at an ordinary coil spring through a microscope almost. The wire, if you want to call it that, is ten inches in diameter and the spring coils are twenty feet across. There are sixteen of them radiating out from the core. In operation they all work together in a compression-tension-torsion complex of balance. The shock absorber and ratchet setup is separate for every fifty feet of spring."

What's that crowd up ahead, Harvey? Looks like somebody is hurt…

"Could be. It happens quite often on a project of this size."

Let's get there. I want to see what happened.

"O.K. I hope you don't emphasize this side of the project in your papers though. It's inevitable, in spite of all safety precautions."

Don't worry. That has been hashed over already enough so that it would be stale reading in my articles.

We hurried forward and pushed through the crowd. Instinctively I pulled back. Then I felt myself turning a distinct shade of green.

It was a particularly nasty accident. A large fabrication had toppled over and caught three men, cutting one completely in two at the waist, a second partly in half so that the upper and lower parts of his torso were held together only on about a third of his right side.

The third man had his left shoulder pinned under a corner of the thing and was conscious. When I got there he was screaming in a heart rending way. Suddenly he stopped that and his features seemed to relax. The next moment he was smiling at someone standing near me, just like nothing was the matter. I thought his mind must have snapped, I mentioned it to Harvey.

"No, Les. I think his screaming was from fear—rather than pain. You don't feel any pain from a thing like that. Not for an hour or two afterwards, at least. He just now realized that he is in no more danger and will certainly live. Now he will be all right."

A siren sounded above the shrill of the metal saws and the constant thunder of heavy mauls against metal and the whine of the overhead cranes. It was the ambulance coming as closely to the scene of the accident as it could. So vast was this gigantic workshop that there was a network of streets about a quarter of a block apart.

Above us a traveling crane had come to a stop, Workers were quickly attaching vise clamps to the thing that had done the damage, so as to lift it off the floor.

The man who was only partly cut in half died while I watched him. I'll never forget the play of expression on his face during that last moment of life. At first there was a dumb wonder mixed with voiceless protest and just a little undercurrent of fear.

His eyes were bloodshot. He turned his head so that it took in the crowds of people that had gathered. For an instant I would have sworn his eyes looked directly into mine, then they passed.

Then his head stopped turning. A smile came to his lips. During that moment I felt that I could read his every thought as easily as I am aware of my own. He seemed to be looking over the shop—his place of work. He was glorying in the knowledge that here he was a God, playing his part in the destiny of America, making things that, when all put together, were a space ship that would travel to the moon and to other planets.

He seemed immensely content with the knowledge that he was dying while doing a man's work—a God's work. Space travel has been so common in fiction for so many years and so many people have read so much of it that we are prone to think of it as an accomplished fact, and belittle the effort being made to bring it about.

Believe me, when I stood there with that huge overhead crane poised above my head, the acres upon acres of work slabs and dirty, hard-working men surrounding me, and the square block or so of the under belly of the huge ship itself showing a couple of hundred feet away over the heads of the men gathered around, the illusion of the commonplace left, and I saw this hive of industry and miracle creation for what it really is: the striving of the human race to fulfill its destiny out in the stars.

I saw the light of life depart from the bloodshot eyes of Grover Rand, for that was the name of that man. At the last it was a light of pride. Pride in the part he had in this gigantic undertaking.

After he died I looked around at the crowd. They were quiet. They had seen what I had seen and been equally aware of those thoughts in that dying man.

I seemed to be seeing them as they really were now. Before, they had been just a sea of dirty, grimy, hardworking men. But now—this one might have been a teller in a bank if he took a bath and put on a white shirt and business suit. That one could very well have been a priest. The one standing on the edge of the nearest slab with a ten pound maul in his right fist might very well have been a surgeon in an operating room with a scalpel held daintily in his skilled fingers.

These were all men—the same as you and I. And those of them who have died, and who may yet die before that huge ship is ready for the Great Adventure, have given their lives for us just as bravely and just as heroically as any soldier on a Pacific beach ever did.

(Don't miss the second article in this series by Les Turner in tomorrow's paper).

Heading:

Space Ship; (AP) Everett, Wa.

March 6, 1943;

Les Turner.

(This is the second in the series of articles by Les Turner on the space ship now nearing completion at Everett Washington. These articles will appear daily for an indefinite period. Don't miss them!)

I ended yesterday on a sad note, but I did so for a definite purpose. First impressions are often impossible to recapture later on, and as a reporter I wanted to give to you as nearly as possible the same feelings and reactions that I myself experienced.

My first impressions continue. This thing is too BIG to get used to in one visit. There is so much that one's eyes just can't register at all.

Getting back to the sequence of events in my yesterday's visit, after the ambulance had carried away the injured man and his two less fortunate fellow workers, Lt. Harvey Dortmer and I, followed by Private Gerald Stone with my portable wire recorder continued on toward the section of the shop directly under the ship.

Here every fifty feet or so was a twenty foot square block of solid concrete which held the underskin of the huge ship off the ground and about twenty feet over our heads.

We were now in the area where finished fabrication was stored, awaiting their sequence in the business of installation. We walked between rows of thousands upon thousands of strange shapes, each with its number which told the initiate what it was and on what part of the ship it went.

Small mobile hoists, called Cherry Pickers, according to Lt. Dortmer, followed young giants like obedient dogs as they wandered in search of wanted parts. When the parts were located they were lifted and carried to the loading platform that surrounded the bank of huge freight elevators that climbed into the ship itself.

I noticed as we drew near this area that although some of the elevators were loading parts and ascending into the ship, to come back empty, most of them were going up empty and coming back loaded with other metal parts, so that on the whole more seemed to be coming out of the ship than was going into it. I asked Lt. Dortmer about this.

WHY is more going out than in?

"About ninety per cent of the ship is completed now, Les. The process of tearing out the skeleton work put in to give the workers platforms upon which to reach their work is going on in those completed sections.

"All this work is planned in sequence and must live up to a schedule. Today is March fifth. On September twentieth, unless some major setback throws the whole thing off, everything will be finished and all the construction equipment will be out."

You mean a job like this that has never been done before can be planned like clockwork?

"I wouldn't say it's never been done before. All the tasks HAVE been done before—in building battleships, bombers, previous space ships, and other things. The time it takes a certain group of workmen to build and install any part of the ship, including time for unforeseen delays, can be figured out according to rules. So much welding will take so long. So much time will be consumed in fitting a part into place. So much time will be consumed and so many delays encountered in getting the part to the spot where it goes."

We entered a small passenger elevator much like those found in office buildings. It was at one end of the bank of freight elevators and much faster.

I was disappointed when we ascended into the interior of the ship. I had expected to see vast stretches of emptiness with a small sphere suspended by giant springs over a thousand feet up.

Instead, I couldn't see over three hundred feet in any direction, because of the working platforms. The elevator climbed five hundred feet and then stopped. We stepped out of it and into a second one which carried us another five hundred feet. A third elevator carried us the rest of the way to the heart of the ship.

There were other elevators that went up further. Here, at the fifteen hundred foot level, we were only half way to the top. It was from this upper section that the skeleton work was being dismantled and taken out.

When we left the elevator we walked along a catwalk with a metal floor and a rail on either side. I stopped and looked over the edge. The distance to the bottom was too great for dizziness. It was like looking at something on the ground from an airplane rather than like looking over the edge on the roof of a skyscraper.

When we stepped into the central sphere it was exactly like stepping below decks on a navy ship. All metal conventional construction with everything covered by glass wool sheets and painted with a sterile looking white.

We were met at once by what seemed to me to be almost a boy. He was a young man, certainly not over twenty-five. When Lt. Dortmer introduced him as Dr. Tziek I couldn't believe it.

Dr. Tziek? I hope you'll pardon me, but I had expected you to be an old man.

He smiled tolerantly.

"That's quite all right. You'll find that Dr. Janes is no older. I'm twenty-six and he's twenty-eight. He intended to be here to meet you with me, but his presence was needed at the power installations up on top. I know you're more interested in knowing what will run the ship than in the navigation instruments, but if you like I'll show you around in my department while you're waiting for him."

You're wrong about my being more interested in the drive principle. I've been told that the navigation instruments are based on new principles, and that they are the big hope for the success of this ship. My readers are probably more curious about them than anything else.

(During this conversation we were walking, and we now stepped into a room that was figuratively and literally JAMMED with all sorts of installations).

"Most of this stuff is radar, radio, and the operating control for the ship. The real heart of all this equipment is this circular table in the center. You see three telescope eye pieces that are attached to black box-like things a foot deep, four inches wide, and four feet long.

"Two of these are at right angle to each other horizontally, and the third points downward. Beside each on the table is a keyboard like that on an adding machine.

"These are three ether-drift measuring instruments. Essentially they are blocks of glass with two silvered surfaces twelve inches apart and perfectly parallel. Light from a projected image at one end enters at almost right angles to one of the mirror surfaces. Then it reflects back and forth from one mirror to the other until it gets to the other end, where it focuses on a small screen, thence into a magnifier.

"The slightest ether velocity will shift the position of the screen image as seen in the telescope, and the amount of that shift is the measure of the ether velocity. The three instruments give us the velocity for three directions at right angles to one another, and the data is fed into a central calculating machine which gives out the actual velocity of the ether and the direction it is flowing.

"This is coordinated with the same measurements for the weight of a piece of metal and the direction in which the metal is pulled.

"Now, in order for you and your readers to understand what all this means, I want you to consider what Einstein said about acceleration. He said that if a man were in a box out in space away from gravity, and the box were accelerating thirty-two feet per second, although there is no gravity field he would weigh the same as if he were on Earth, and wouldn't be able to tell the difference.

"That's what happens to the weight. BUT under such a setup there would be no gravity field, and the ether drift instruments wouldn't register, so Einstein was wrong when he said there was no way to distinguish between weight due to gravity and weight due to acceleration. The four instruments at this table do just that, and give the acceleration of the ship relative to the ether, and also the speed of the ship through the ether.

THE speed of the ship THROUGH the ether is the most important fact we must know at all times in space flight. It's the factor that has defeated space travel up to now, because

WITHOUT TAKING THAT FACTOR INTO CONSIDERATION THE SPEED AND DIRECTION OF THE SHIP CANNOT BE CONTROLLED."

How does that affect it? Of course I know that ether drift produces gravity attraction. Everybody knows that now, and that the gravity here on Earth that makes me weigh a hundred and eighty-four pounds is due to ether rushing through me at the speed of eighty-eight plus miles per second.

But out in space, how does it affect the course of the ship? The planets drift around in it without any trouble, and the astronomers can predict where they will be for centuries ahead, right to the second.

"Of course. Because they are drifting with the ether, so to speak. The space ship won't be doing that, though. It will be bucking ether currents all the time. If we ran out of fuel we would slow down or speed up until we were just like a bit of bark floating on a stream. Our course would be quite predictable, but we couldn't control it.

"I'll give you a practical example. Suppose we were in this ship out in space. We come near the Earth and set up what we suppose to be a stable orbit around the Earth, about a thousand miles up. If we travel the same direction as the moon is going the orbit WILL be stable; but if we go in the opposite direction our forward speed will decelerate a few inches each second and we will get closer and closer to the atmosphere, until finally we plunge into it."

You said this group of instruments will give the velocity of the ship relative to the ether?

"Yes, but don't confuse that with absolute motion. The ether itself is always on the move. In the solar system it moves in a pattern much like a whirlpool, in the plane of the ecliptic. The Earth is the center of another such whirlpool, and that whirlpool makes the rotation of the Earth on its axis every day.

"The moon started the Earth's whirlpool in the first place, and keeps it spinning. ONLY PLANETS OR MOONS WITH SIZEABLE SATELLITES ROTATE ON THEIR AXIS. AND ALWAYS IN THE SAME DIRECTION AS THE SATELLITE THAT BEARS A CLOSE RELATIONSHIP TO THE FACTORS OF THE SATELLITES' ORBIT.

"That fact used to be taken to prove that the satellites were thrown off from the central body, but it is now known that the solar system would have about the same configuration it now has if all the individual planets and moons were brought together by chance!

"Even the spiral nebulae prove it. The individual stars in the spiral nebulae are an average distance of ten light years apart, and there are millions of them in one nebula, yet the overall pattern of the nebula is that of a whirlpool, or vortex. It used to be thought that this was due to the stars condensing from a more or less uniform cloud of gas, and since the gas had a rotary motion, it followed that the condensation would also have the same motion. That theory made it seem that the spiral nebulae were young and tem-porary, and it postulated the necessity for huge atmospheres of uniformly distributed gas that were fifteen or twenty thousand light years across. Now we know that the spiral nebulae are permanent aggregates, and have been in much their present state for untold billion; and trillions of centuries, and that there is no reason why they should ever change much in overall outline."

AT that moment another young man stepped into the control room. He was introduced to me as Dr. Janes. Both he and Dr. Tziek were of medium build, blond, and had a scholarly appearance. They reminded me more of college students than scientists. Although I had seen pictures of them before it was somewhat of a shock to an old man of forty to realize that the greatest show on Earth was being masterminded by two kids under thirty.

However I didn't waste time on personalities right then. The secret of how this ship was going to be driven was what I wanted most, and I went right to the point.

I have a portable recorder with me, Doctor Jane. The world is waiting with its tongue hanging out for information on how this ship is to run with no rocket jets. Suppose you start explaining to me now, and we can continue on that while you show me around the power setup.

"That sounds all right to me, Mr. Turner—er, Les. To begin with, we'll have to go back to the nature of the electron and the proton. Also the neutron and other basic particles. We'll stick to the electron and the proton for simplicity.

"It used to be thought that the electron, for example, had two things; (1) an electric charge, and (2) a gravitational mass. The electric charge was supposed to give rise to the electric field, and the mass evidenced itself as inertia when the electron was in motion, and as a gravity field at all times. The same went for the proton except that the mass and gravity field about the proton were over a thousand times that of the electron.

"We now know that the proton is a very complex unit instead of the simple thing we used to think it was. We also know that a gravitational field is a neutralized electrical field, and that inertial mass is only indirectly related to strength of field. It's all rather complex unless you sit down and learn the basics step by step.

"What I've been leading up to is simply this: inertial mass is of two kinds just as electric charge is of two kinds— positive and negative. In nature things are so much in balance that the forces we deal with are always residues. For example, a ton of lead is thought to have a ton of inertial mass. Actually it has several tons of one kind of inertial mass and one ton more or less than that of the other kind, so that the residue after most of the actual mass has cancelled out is a ton.

"In the same way the gravity field strength of a ton of lead is almost too weak for any possible measurement, yet it is a neutralization of two equal electrical fields whose individual strengths if separated would rival the attraction of the sun in pulling power!

"Getting back to this idea of two kinds of inertial mass, let's picture two different bullets made of pure inertial mass, each of one kind. The recoil of the gun when one is fired would be in the direction opposite to that of the flight of the bullet, while for the other it would be in the direction the bullet went.

"We use this principle to drive the ship. Instead of shooting matter out of a tube and using the recoil to drive the ship forward we use electricity and shoot the protons out of the bottom of the ship and the electrons out of the top, all at the same time. That way we use nearly the full inertial mass to drive the ship instead of a residue.

"We don't have to carry a supply of matter to use up in this way, either. That's where the real value of the tremendous area of the outer shell comes in. In flight through space this area collects the electrons and positrons and protons from the space we pass through!

OUR power plant draws them in and separates them, driving the positive electricity sternward and the negative electricity forward. It shoots them away from the ship at speeds that are nearly a third of the speed of light—far greater than rocket gasses could attain!

"Now I'm going to let you in on a little secret, Les. You and the public. It takes very little power to do all this. The maximum that our power plant can develop is fifteen thousand horsepower. That's less than that developed by the power plant of a large bomber, and it is more than twice enough to lift us away from the Earth.

"We get our energy from an atomic pile. It could go on generating that maximum power continuously for several thousand years, so this ship could hop from one planet to another, leave the solar system behind and go to the nearest stars and come back again, and never need refueling until this age we live in has become a small part of ancient history or even of pre-history, if some cataclysm were to destroy written records."

* * *

Irwin Crabtree laid the report down at this point and flicked the switch to Venus Central on his desk.

"To Dr. J. R. Boniface, Custodian of the Archives. Dear Dr. Boniface: Some of the contents of the material seem not only significant to my study, but also point to the existence of certain other items. These would be Q559 G432 and Q559 G447. Please rush this. Yours truly, Dr. I. S. Crabtree."

After the operator repeated the message he broke the connection. For nearly an hour he remained motionless except for the occasional drumming of his fingers on the desk. He ignored the rest of the report on the desk before him.

There was a discreet knock at the door. A messenger came in with several photostat sheets. Irwin took them and glanced hastily through them. Then he grunted with satisfaction and started to read them carefully.

The first one was headed Item; Section Q559 0432. It read:

U.N. Capitol, New York:—A bill was introduced in the assembly this morning by Soviet Minister Dashski designed to prohibit the annexation of soil on the moon or any other planet by any nation by right of discovery, and to impose immediate penalties of a drastic nature on any nation that attempted to set up rocket installations on the moon.

This was obviously aimed at crippling the present plans of the United States which hinge on the success of the ship which is ready for departure on its maiden voyage to the Moon.

The United States promptly vetoed the introduction of the bill, When the Soviet Minister heard this veto he rose and shouted that if the United States did not rescind its veto and permit discussion of the bill his country would be compelled to consider the United Nations an ineffective instrument and withdraw.

The U.S. Minister promptly reminded the Soviet Minister that he was out of order, and that the precedent for veto had been well established by the Soviet representatives. If they now withdrew when it was used against them it would have to be construed by the United States as a declaration of war by the Soviet against the United Nations and the United States.

The Soviet Minister retorted that the veto of the United States on this matter could be construed in no other way by his country than a declaration of hostile intent and that he was instructed by his government in the case of a veto by the United States to make a statement. He then read from a prepared statement, "In the event of a veto by the United States on this bill the Union of Soviet Socialist Republics must consider such veto as tantamount to a direct declaration of hostilities by that government, and will henceforth act accordingly."

Then, white of face and in a strained voice, the Soviet Minister added, "This is the unalterable position of my government. The next move is up to the United States Minister."

Thereupon the United States Minister rose and stated that he would have to confer with his government on the matter, and asked for a recess until tomorrow when he would either reaffirm his veto or withdraw it, according to whatever instructions he received.

IRWIN turned to the next sheet and frowned when he saw it was headed 447. That meant that there was no record of the next day's session of the U.N. Council. Still frowning, he read on:

Section Q559 G447: BOOK OF THE WEEK. (A weekly review of an outstanding book by Giles Rupert, noted author and critic, written especially for this paper). The book, Suspended Animation, by Dr. G. W. Hines, physiologist at the Mayo clinic, is destined to become a best seller. Four hundred pages long, it deals with every phase of the problem from types of suspended animation found in nature to laboratory successes in this subject with human guinea pigs. It attempts to get at the explanations as well as the techniques, and even draws on legend and history for possible incidents, advancing logical theories to account for these ancient tales.

The book is divided into three parts. In the first, hibernation is dealt with, together with well authenticated cases where cold blooded animals have been sealed up for decades without dying. In the second section sleeping sickness and artificially induced hibernation of warm blooded animals is discussed.

The last section of the book is most, fascinating. General theories about sleep and unconsciousness, and also about suspended bodily function, are built into a gripping whole. Tales of vampires from the middle ages are discussed in the light of present findings. Problems to be overcome before successful suspended animation can become a fact are outlined and possible laboratory procedure is given.

Were vampires really dead, or in suspended animation? Could there be a physiological explanation that might give credence to the very elaborate tales concerning human vampires that flourished in Europe and elsewhere three to five centuries ago? The discussion of this problem in the book will grip the reader far more than the most hair raising of fiction stories ever could.

If you want a book that you can't lay, down, this is it.

THERE were over thirty items in this classification. None of the others seemed of any value. The book had not been sent to Venus through the television broadcasts from the Earth expedition.

Irwin glanced at his watch. Time to get back to the telescope again. With Mars rotating in one direction and the sphere moving in the other it didn't take long for it to circle the planet relative to one spot.

He laid the papers in a neat pile on one side of his desk and left the room, retracing his steps to the observatory proper. An assistant had already turned the huge frame so that it pointed toward the spot on the horizon where the sphere was expected to reappear.

At the precise second calculated, it jumped into sight. It climbed into the sky rapidly at first. Then a change took place. The one pole visible in the telescope grew almost incandescent. The sphere disappeared and Irwin had to disconnect the clock drive and wait a few seconds, then operate the drive by push button control to keep it in view.

Unbelievable deceleration was taking place in that ship. Three hours later it settled into the first layers of atmosphere. After that it grew in the telescope until even a small insect could have been brought into focus on its surface.

There was no need to flash the alarm. The sounds of people shouting could be heard all over the city of Orno.

The unsuspected power of the mystery ship had upset the calculations of the observatory mathematicians, but their prediction of the spot where the ship would land was correct.

Irwin Crabtree called the local police and issued terse orders. He had prepared for this moment days before and received emergency power over all local government on his insistence that it might mean the difference between survival and extinction.

It took him five minutes of precious time to reach the exit to the observatory building. By then a police car was waiting for him. He climbed in and the machine picked up speed rapidly, its exhaust whistle shrilling loudly.

Cars pulled over along the way in response to the police whistle hooked into the exhaust so that it took very little time to reach the valley where the huge sphere was now settling.

Other police cars were scurrying around and stopping at strategic positions where they could prevent the crowd that was beginning to collect from going down into the valley and approaching the ship.

Dr. Crabtree's eyes were feverish with excitement. Was this the same ship that had left the Earth so long ago? He felt it must be. Had the original crew managed to remain alive in suspended animation all this time? He felt that that must be impossible; but perhaps the present crew were descendants of the original crew, just as he was certain the people of Mars and Venus were the descendants of the original passengers this same ship had left on the two planets.

In a little while he should know. With hands that shook he unfurled a white flag he had ordered for the car. He hung this out the side window so it could be seen plainly from the ship, and ordered the driver to approach the ship slowly.

The car crept down the switchback road into the valley. Twenty minutes later it stopped just even with the outer bulge of the fantastic sphere.

HE opened the car door to climb out onto the ground. A strange freak of circumstance saved his life. The car had stopped near a mound of dirt. As the car door swung open it came to within an inch of this mound. There was a blinding flash of electricity as the charge that had accumulated in the car body discharged into the soil.

"Of course!" Irwin Crabtree exclaimed as the explanation for this flashed into his mind. He hesitated, wondering if any charge remained. Then he remembered his electronics and stepped boldly onto the ground with the white flag firmly held erect in front of him.

The electric flash had been due to the accumulation in the tire-insulated car body of positrons and protons shot out of the ship to cushion its fall. Those that had struck the soil had immediately attracted electrons from all over so that the earth charge had become neutral. Those that had struck the car had been held like a charge on a condenser plate until the car door had formed a small enough gap for the charge to escape.

Conscious of the thousands of eyes that were watching him from the surrounding hills, Dr. Crabtree slowly approached the ship over the uneven ground.

The air was highly charged, and a faint ozone smell coupled with a strange odor of burnt metal accentuated the feeling of alienness about the ship. Its size defied the senses.

There was no faintest sound from the gigantic globe, yet it had an aura of titanic, living strength.

Irwin Crabtree looked up at the smooth surface that bulged outward and into the sky above, and thought, "That surface has been exposed for thousands of years to the cold and sterile vacuum of interstellar space and is as perfect as the day it first received its finishing polish. What a perfect, indestructible metal it must be!"

Immediately ahead of him a circular opening appeared and a rope ladder dropped out with an unrolling motion, to touch the ground with a yard to spare.

Irwin stood still, the stick of his white flag digging into his trousers belt as he held the flag upright. Behind him he could hear the television truck maneuvering for position so that it could bring to two worlds the first sight of these beings from some other star. The public did not yet know of Irwin's suspicions that this ship had originally come from Earth.

Fifteen minutes went by. Then a half hour. Still no movement came from the round opening in the bottom of the ship.

A messenger came up behind him and handed him a note. It was from the Mayor of Orno suggesting that two policemen be sent up the ladder. He had two volunteers. After some hesitation Irwin wrote a simple "Very well" on the back of the note and handed it back to the messenger.

A moment or two later two young men in the universal bright red of the constabulary of Mars approached Irwin, clicked their heels smartly, and saluted.

He returned the salute and outlined his plan.

"I have a pretty good idea of what we will find in there," he said. "For several reasons I feel it would be better if I went with you. One of you will precede me up the ladder and the other will follow me and give me any assistance I may need."

"Very well, sir," one of them said, acting as spokesman for the both of them.

The three advanced to the foot of the dangling rope ladder. Without hesitation one of the bright red figures rapidly scaled the ladder. Then Dr. Crabtree followed, more slowly, while the third figure kept the ladder from swaying. When the aged astronomer had disappeared through the opening into the ship, he followed.

After the three disappeared from sight through the dark opening the gathering thousands of people settled down to wait.

The television truck had brought the whole thing to the populations of both Mars and Venus far more clearly than those on the surrounding hills could see it. But now, as time passed, those on the scene began to experience the strange, subduing, alien interstellarness of the ship—its air of cauterized, infinite power, and contempt of attack.

The sun dipped below the horizon. Still the throngs waited, and still the three men did not return. But with darkness a dim glow could be seen emerging through the opening in the ship.

PART TWO

IRWIN Crabtree stepped off the rope ladder onto a small platform inside the huge sphere. His darting eyes took in the immensity of space above him and the details of the ship as revealed by a uniform dim glow that pervaded the very atmosphere, as it seemed.

Fifteen hundred feet above was a smaller sphere. It looked like the bloated belly of a huge spider sitting in the center of its web, with the huge coil springs radiating out from it in all directions to the outer shell.

Beside the platform upon which he stood was a large elevator. A fragile, quarter-inch strand of woven metal went up from its roof to become a faint line that disappeared within a hundred yards because of smallness and lack of lustre.

Evidently they were expected to travel in this elevator into the upper sections of the sphere.

Curious as to how the elevator was designed. Irwin stepped into it. A pipe ran from the roof to the floor in the exact center of the elevator. Obviously the thin strand of wire rope up which the elevator was to ride must pass through this pipe and be anchored to the shell of the sphere. In some way the elevator gained traction as well as support from that single strand.

He motioned for the two police to follow him. The instant all three were safely in, the door closed and the elevator started to rise. Was this due to automatic mechanism built into the elevator? Or did some person or being above start it as soon as he saw they were in? Why had they not been met?

Irwin shoved these questions into the back of his mind. They would be answered eventually, and speculation about them now was fruitless.

The elevator rose steadily with a faint hum coming from the center pipe. The flatness of the shell below rapidly assumed a concave appearance, and the ship core gradually lost its appearance of being a living thing crouching in a web far above and began to look like what it was—the actual space ship, of which the three thousand foot outer sphere was just a protective shield and gatherer of cosmic particles for fuel for the propulsion mechanism.

The elevator was slow. After the first few minutes the novelty of the thing wore off. The two policemen introduced themselves. They were George Hanson and Fred Brown.

"If you will pardon me for saying so, sir," George said respectfully after their introductions, "I've noticed that you seem to know more about this ship than if you had never heard of it before."

"That's right," Irwin said. "There's an account of a ship just like this being built on the Earth. I got the account just today from the Archives. Either this is the same ship, or else there is only one way to build a successful space ship, so that anyone who went from some other solar system to this one would have to build one like it to succeed. I don't know which is the case, but we should find out soon. I imagine the captain of this ship is waiting up there impatiently for the elevator to reach its destination."

"I hope they're friendly," Fred Brown said fervently.

"There's no reason why they shouldn't be," Irwin assured him. "After all, beings intelligent enough to build a ship like this aren't out for savage, senseless killing. They probably haven't shown themselves because it would be much more probable that WE are the savage creatures, and they wouldn't want to trust themselves to our mercy until they have seen a sample of what we are."

"That must be it," Fred said, reassured.

The central sphere was now beginning to show its size. The elevator had swung over and was rising directly underneath it. The thin strand of cable could be traced into an opening in the bottom now.

The small opening far below in the outer shell, through which the three men had entered the ship, had become no more than a pin point of light.

There were noises—the hum of the elevator mechanism, a quiet high speed hum, and the voices of the men when they spoke. The steady noises had a non-directional quality to them that made them seem a part of the atmosphere rather than sounds. The voices had a strange way of repeating themselves quite distinctly and loudly. All this strangeness of sound was due to its being confined inside a huge shell which reflected it back.

THE elevator roof reached the opening into the central sphere and stopped. Next it rotated about its supporting cable until two grooves on opposite sides of the elevator were in line with two guide rails in the shaft. After that it rose again, the grooves of the elevator slipping over the guide rails with a slight settling bounce.

The vastness of the outer sphere was immediately replaced by the close normalcy of a conventional elevator.

A door dropped slowly past the rising car. There were transparent windows in it that revealed a long corridor. The view slipped below the car floor. Twenty more such scenes slipped slowly by to tantalize the whetted curiosity of the three men before the car finally stopped.

This time the door in the shaft slid open invitingly. The three men stepped out into a large room. Facing them about twenty feet away were a dozen young men, a friendly smile on their faces, but a wary look in their eyes as if they were ready for a first hostile act from the visitors.

Dr. Crabtree took in all this and said quietly to the two policemen, "Don't do anything unless I tell you to."

Then he stepped forward, his white flag held at his side and a disarming smile on his lips.

He spoke in the ancient root language of Mars and Venus.

"Welcome to Mars," he said simply. "I am Dr. Irwin Crabtree of the astronomical observatory here at Orno."

The strange ship dwellers looked at one another, pleased surprise on their faces. Then advanced with hand outstretched.

"This IS a surprise," he said, pumping Irwin's hand enthusiastically. "Then the colony our ancestors left on Mars took root. Since you speak English with only a slight distortion of pronunciation it must be that the ancient knowledge was not lost in your climb through the centuries."

"It was largely lost," Irwin said sadly. "But we gained it back again. The colony on Venus has done just as well. We are in constant communication by radio, although we don't have space flight."

The other star travelers were lining up to shake hands with the three Martians. They obviously considered this in the nature of a homecoming.

THEY were surprised to find the two red clad policemen couldn't understand their speech. Irwin explained that modern Martian was quite a bit different than the ancient root tongue, and that he had learned English from the old writings, giving it the modern Martian pronunciation because he knew no other.

"Aren't there more of you than this? Irwin finally asked.

"Oh, yes," one of the twelve men replied. "We number fifteen thousand. We here are what you might call a suicide squad. The rest are watching this room through the inter-communication system, but this room is sealed. It's necessary to find out several things before we can mix freely. The state of civilization you have is one thing. We want to know whether we are going to have to be careful lest some ambitious Martian tries to steal the ship and become ruler of everything he can lay his hands on. The most vital thing we must find out, though, is whether we are carriers of any disease that might be harmful if released on Mars and whether you have acquired new diseases that might kill off all of us before we could stop it."

"Hmm," Erwin said thoughtfully, "So that is the two reasons you didn't communicate with us or come out to meet us. It might very well have been the end of you. Did you know that when you first started circling the planet we tried to destroy you because you wouldn't give us any kind of reply to our broadcasts hurled at you?"

"Oh, that!" The man laughed indulgently. "Planetlubbers—that's what we call people who have never been away from a planet, have exaggerated ideas of the strength of the forces they command. Don't get me wrong, though. We know how destructive the cyclotron beam can be. But our ship uses such things for fuel and your attack was to our ship what an extra helping of food at a meal would be to your body. We ignored it."

"Is this the ship that was built on the Earth in 1953?" Irwin asked suddenly.

"The same one," the man replied, "When it dropped off colonizers on Venus and Mars the original crew of men and women decided to explore the rest of the solar system. After a few years of that they left for the region of Sirius, the Dog Star. Our power plant was good for several thousands of years. It would be at least two thousand years before Earth became habitable again; the colonies were doing all right and would eventually cover both Mars and Venus, but in that long struggle ahead there would undoubtedly be a recapitulation of Earth history; and they had the ship with which to reach the stars. So they left it all behind, to hatch, you might say. Now we have returned to see what kind of chicks resulted."

"But what happened on Earth?" Irwin asked. "What took place that made the home planet uninhabitable?"

"It's along story," the man answered. "We are going to have a little celebration dinner in honor of you, our first guests since our return home. After that you'll get the story. By the way, Dr. Crabtree, my name is Jack Janes."

"Janes!" exclaimed Irwin. "Then you are a direct descendant of the man who invented the power drive on this ship!"

"Of course!" Jack said. "We all are. In the course of several hundred generations starting with a hundred couples it is inevitable that everyone is a direct descendant of all those of the first generation."

"Of course," Irwin chuckled. "I hadn't thought of that."

"We have had to enforce strict marriage rules here that would never be necessary on a planet," Jack went on. "First of all was birth control because the population had no room for expansion. Next came systematic laws on what we called the principle of remotest relation. It's more complex than you would think. It was necessary to prevent inbreeding and the consequent weakening of the stock."

"I am not too well acquainted with genetics," Irwin said, "but I get what you mean. I gather the young man was told that he had five or six eligible girls to choose from and no more?"

"That's right," Jack said. "Sometimes it is only one. No choice. But here comes the food."

A door had opened revealing another large room in which a long table was set. The twelve men and their three Martian guests took their seats.

The two policemen, George and Fred, had been rapidly catching onto the ancient language that was so much like their own. Also they had been getting acquainted with the other men and finding them very much to their liking.

The meal began with three capsules and a glass of a sparkling beverage of strange flavor.

Jack began the meal by picking up the capsules on his plate and holding them up. "These are vitamins," he explained. "Do you know what they are?"

"Oh, yes," Irwin replied. "We discovered vitamins several centuries ago. But we call them controls."

"Well, we'll get you on the food," Jack said good naturedly. "I'll bet you've never heard of half the vegetables on this table, have you?"

Irwin looked over the collection of food-stuffs. There wasn't a single familiar vegetable.

"You have the advantage of me now," he said with a twinkle.

"I should," Jack said. "You see, we have little original work we can do except create new varieties of plants, and that has been one of our main interests for generations. The names and parentage of them won't mean much to you. Eat them and see how they taste. There'll be plenty of time from now on to learn what they are."

An hour later the fifteen men sat back and prepared to listen to Jack tell the story of the end of life on Earth, and how his ancestors had rescued a remnant of humanity and planted it on Mars and Venus.

To Jack and his eleven companions of the "suicide" squad it was an old story learned during their early childhood. To George Hanson and Fred Brown, the two red clad policemen it was a partly understood tale in a curious distortion of their own language. But to Irwin it was the final answer to the enigma that had puzzled two worlds for centuries. He listened breathlessly.

"In 1945," Jack began, "the first atom bomb was used to end a world war. In all, in 1945 and 1947 there were five such bombs exploded. The men who created these bombs did not concern themselves with the possible after-effects. They merely made the bomb work successfully. They had a naive confidence in the goodness of nature. They did not realize that chain effects belong to a family of phenomena akin to life. Millions of yeas before that time a certain molecule had come into existence by chance in the hot gases of the cooling Earth. It was the first molecule on Earth possessing the peculiar property of reproducing itself. The RP property, it is called.

"That molecule had perhaps one chance in ten billion of reproducing rather than being destroyed in a chemical action with its environment. Perhaps ten billion had already been created and destroyed before this one succeeded. It DID reproduce itself, again and again. Up to a certain point in numbers of descendants of this first successful life form the chances of its continuance were slim. On Mars and Venus and perhaps other members of the solar system this same thing took place. The planets were cooling, and before long the conditions necessary for the spontaneous creation of this first life form would be gone. It was nip and tuck, with the odds about ten to one against its success, but it did succeed, and life established itself on the Earth.

"Eventually there were thousands of billions of these first living molecules. Thousands of them were being destroyed by environment every minute, and more thousands were coming into existence from the ones that weren't destroyed, until the odds against survival disappeared entirely.

"Now, sometimes environment in destroying one of these molecules produced what is known as a mutation. In other words, a living molecule that couldn't have been created spontaneously, and a little more complex than the first form. Perhaps there were only one or two possible mutations to the first form. However many there were, eventually all of them came into existence.

AS the Earth cooled and environment changed and all the possible mutations on the first life forms came into existence, these in turn took all the possibilities opened up to them in mutation.

"The failures—the unsuccessful mutations, were destroyed by environment. The successes spread out mutationally in all directions, being pruned back and directed by environment just as the banks of a stream on a planet direct that stream to the ocean. Step by step life became more complex, less complex, more stable, and less stable, going upward and downward in the scale of evolution and also standing still, so that in 1945 when the atom bomb was first used the original molecular chain reaction had produced man and his intelligent brain. That, from a beginning as a simple molecule in a chemical reaction.

"The reason I'm telling you all this is to show you what consequences can come from such simple beginnings. If there had been entities on the Earth in that beginning of life to whom life would be fatal, and if that first molecule with the RP property had been produced by one of those entities, he would have had to be almost infinitely wise to foresee the ultimate consequences of his scientific work. He wouldn't have foreseen, of course. The consequences were too subtle, only becoming obvious after millions of years and through millions of imperceptible developments.

"The chain reaction in the atomic pile is an RP action. One neutron hits a heavy atom and results in more than one neutron. The reproduction of free neutrons is the chain reaction, analogous to life, and is the principle of the atom bomb.

"These free neutrons by the billions were let loose in the atmosphere with each explosion, and in the atmosphere they encountered a new environment. No mutation was possible, since a neutron is a neutron always, unless it is safely captured by the nucleus of an atom that remains stable with its acquisition. These "deaths" of the neutrons were more than outnumbered by the reproduction of a neutron by collision with some gas atom that split and let loose two or more neutrons.

"The increase was slow. After 1947 it was beyond recall, but it wouldn't become obvious for two or three more centuries, just as the results from the creation of the first life form—a simple molecule able to reproduce itself, could not have been seen on the Earth to any great extent until millions of years later.

"But with the war over and peace talks going on indefinitely, one of the scientists sat back and did a little thinking and got the right answer. He immediately went to the President and in the course of events it was proven he was right.

"If he had been wrong—IF SUCH A CHAIN REACTION IN THE ATMOSPHERE HAD NOT BEEN A REALITY BUT MERELY A FICTION, perhaps the history of atomic explosives would have taken the same course as the history of dynamite and become just one of the stock weapons of nations in their perpetual battles.

"As it was the government had two courses it could follow. It could carve out safe places under the surface where a large part of the people could go. And/or it could try to build successful space ships and go to other planets.

"It attempted both courses. The move into the underground was kept secret but the space ship couldn't be secret. After many failures this ship was built. The first ships had used the rocket principle, and their only value had been to prove the inadequacy of the basics of science and compel their revision.

"This ship made its maiden voyage to the moon and returned successfully. But while it was gone other nations had decided that the United States must be destroyed before she built rocket bomb stations on the moon that could dominate the entire Earth.

"They didn't have atom bombs, but they DID have radioactives, and they spread them by the ton all over the

United States from rockets in the stratosphere. It was a stupid, psychological attack from start to finish. The radioactives were merely ordinary Uranium which is relatively safe. The scientists of the United States shouted this at the top of their lungs and no one believed them.

AN all out war was inevitable and everyone knew it. This ship was not designed for fighting. The government, fearing the end of civilization was certain, ordered the crew to take on board all the people, books, and equipment that could be carried, and take them to Mars, Venus, and any other place where there might be a chance for survival.

"Then the government made its fatal error. Having on hand over fifty atom bombs, it decided that the war could be ended quickly by destroying the governments of the attackers and dealing with the populations when they were disorganized. They reasoned idealistically that the people didn't want war and that the people loved the United States. The People were the downtrodden masses who were the victims of totalitarianism. They really wanted Democracy if they had a chance to get it.

"Perhaps there were quite a few people in other countries that were like that, but it takes more than quite a few. It takes ninety-nine per cent.

"Anyway, to get back to what happened, this ship left for Venus the same day that Operation Terminal, as it was named, went into operation.

"Our ancestors, yours and mine together, looked back and saw the flashes from those atom bombs. The ship stayed at Venus for six months while the Venusian settlers were getting established. Then it cut across to Mars and stayed there for another six months.

"Then they decided to explore the moons of Jupiter for possible inhabitable ones. Exploration continued until every body in the solar system had been visited. That period is a story in itself, and we have it all in our library.

"Finally our ancestors returned to the Earth. They never were able to find out exactly what had happened there. Civilization was gone and the atmosphere was getting dangerously radioactive. The people in all countries including the United States had degenerated into small colonies and bands of wandering marauders, each a law unto itself. Their eventual end was certain. Extinction.

"Whether the move into the underground had succeeded or not could not be determined. There was nothing to do but leave before radioactive poisons contaminated their bodies.

"Our ancestors went back to Venus. There we found that the original colony had split up into three groups under three different leaders and gone their separate ways. The future there would repeat the history of the Earth. There would be wars and pillage when the populations grew larger.

"On Mars it was the same. The human race was at low ebb, and true civilization remained only in a sphere three thousand feet in diameter.

"It was then the decision to go to Sirius was made. It was fairly certain there were many planets around that star. Also the dense star was a mystery that intrigued them.

"Three years later the ship passed Pluto and began its journey through the void. Only it wasn't so void after all."

Jack stopped talking and looked at his companions with a humorous smile on his face.

"What do you mean it wasn't so void?" Irwin asked.

"Have your psychologists on Venus and Mars solved the principle of the operation of the human brain?" Jack asked.

"Why, I don't believe so," Irwin replied, "Why?"

"They undoubtedly have dissected the brain and also discovered the encephalograph, at least," Jack persisted. "You can't possibly have attained interplanetary television without having someone discover that the brain gives off radio waves capable of influencing a sensitive electronic device placed near the brain."

"Oh, yes," Irwin said, "We have that all right. We know that the brain is a maze of nerve tubes that connect at small nodes, and these nerves originate at certain cells in the cortex. Undoubtedly there have been attempts to figure out what goes on physically in the brain during thinking, but I am not too much up on that."

TOO bad," Jack said regretfully. "But maybe I can get across what I want to say about the brain before going into the subject of interstellar space in a way you can understand.

"The nodes and the connecting nerves of the brain are the memory circuit. The nodes may be likened to small check valves that are stuck closed. A certain amount of fluid pressure breaks them open, and after that they stay open or they close, but will open under the least pressure. In that way the cells in the cortex establish sequences and direct connections with one another.

"This is the automatic mechanism of the brain and comprises sense impressions and the vast sea of the subconscious. It's the vast keyboard and organ of the conscious mind, and is able to operate successfully WITHOUT a conscious mind. In the same way the conscious mind is able to operate WITHOUT THIS BRAIN MECHANISM.

"In this ship, generation after generation, as we have traveled through space, we have definitely proven all that I am telling you. For example, we have proven that certain drugs make the brain completely inoperative temporarily. If thought is the product of the brain alone, then under these drugs there would be no thought and certainly no awareness through the senses.

"Yet the conscious mind, although divorced absolutely from all sense awareness, develops the ability to be aware of things that take place during that period of complete paralysis of the brain function. This has been proven.

"Also it has been proven that the brain can operate successfully without the knowledge of the conscious mind. By hypnosis the conscious mind has been divorced from the brain and exhaustive psychological tests have been made. These have shown the nature of the relation between the function of the brain and the function of the conscious mind.

"These tests have been very exhaustive and have been done so much that error is out of the question. They have proven that the seat of the conscious mind is not in the brain proper, and is not affected by drugs in any way.

"It has been amply demonstrated that the conscious mind can even leave the body entirely for long periods and then return.

"From there on we have mainly theory and necessary conclusion, but no objective proof. But it seems quite certain that the conscious mind and the seat of reasoning, imagination, and a large part of memory itself with emphasis on generalizations and principles, resides in some very small unit which may be a single molecule or even something smaller. Whatever it is, it is unique in nature. Whatever its origin, it seems to be indestructible.

"In interstellar space there are vast swarms of these units, and without exception they all claim to have originated on various planets in some form or other of living organism. Some of them are millions of years old. Others are very young, relatively speaking.

"Together, they comprise a vast civilization of thousands of billions of individual thinking entities! Interstellar space is divided up into districts and regions by them, and they have little concern for solar systems, steering clear of them almost entirely.

"That is what my ancestors found when they left the solar system! Does it sound believable, doctor?"

"I believe anything you tell me," Irwin said seriously. "Still, it is almost beyond belief. The nature of the proofs you have outlined seem to be of a kind that our own scientists could duplicate though. And I'm sure that if you advance your own data they can verify it and support at least the possibility of what you say. It sounds interesting. Your ancestors left a dying civilization and plunged right into the midst of a vast interstellar one far older than the Earth. Is that right?"

"Correct," Jack said. "Oh, it took them over a century to be sure it wasn't space madness and delusion. Eventually they completed the proof of its reality. From then on life on the ship was a great adventure. More than an adventure, really, because OUR ANCESTORS ARE STILL WITH US. Yes. Those original pioneers that left the Earth and left your ancestors here on Mars to go out into the interstellar spaces in the hope that their descendants would reach another star REACHED THAT STAR THEMSELVES. AND HAVE RETURNED.

"What?" Irwin said, sitting up suddenly. "Do you mean they are still alive and on this ship?"

"Not still alive," Jack said, laughing. "But the vehicle that holds the seat of consciousness is still in existence, and is on this ship."

"That sounds to me like ancestor worship," Irwin said, not sure now whether he was being kidded or whether Jack sincerely believed all this.

"Not worship," Jack corrected. "Reverence, yes. Respect too. The same kind of respect I hold for you. But demonstrable fact is not religion."

"You mean I could talk to those ancestors of yours?" Irwin asked.

"I don't know," Jack said doubtfully. "You see, doctor, talking with a spirit is quite a bit different than talking with a language. It takes a natural aptitude and long training to do it. In a way it's a different language entirely through a different sense.

"I'll give you an analogy that will show you the difference. In television the image that goes into the television eye sets up a complicated electric current. This is broadcast and picked up by the receiver, which is designed to convert the current back into the image again. Right?"

"Yes," Irwin answered.

"Suppose that instead of going into a television receiver it were to go into an amplifier and come out as sound. Could your ears pick up the sound and convert it into a visual image in your mind?"

"Hardly," Irwin said.

"It could with training," Jack corrected. "By seeing the image and hearing the sound equivalent to the image you could eventually build up the necessary associations to do it. The image of a man, for example, would produce a sound of a certain kind. Soon you would recognize that sound and associate it with the image.

"Perhaps a simpler illustration would be the sound track on a film. There—"

"I get what you mean now," Irwin said. "We have an instrument for the totally deaf. It's quite common. It converts the sound into a complex sine wave image. The person goes to a school where he learns to read these sine wave images. It's really remarkable. Would you believe it? They actually learn to enjoy music and tonal quality, and those that did have hearing at one time say that after a few years the images of the sounds are converted by the mind into sound again so that they hear with their eyes via the oscillograph!"

"There you have it," Jack said, laughing. "We have instruments that pick up the ether waves set up by these ancestors of ours and amplify them millions of times. They are incredibly delicate. We learn to understand them and recognize them so that eventually most of us don't need the instruments to talk with our ancestors.

"After quarantine is over you'll get a chance to try one of those instruments and see what you get. Some people are natural telepaths without knowing it, and already have learned to interpret these ether waves correctly. If you're one of those you should be able to make sense out of what you get through the instrument."

"You talk of ether waves," Irwin said. "In the account of the building of this ship published in a newspaper at the time there was mention of new basics in science. Yet the nature of those basics was given rather obscurely and certainly aren't known to us. This ether, for example. We have proven there is no ether."

"You mean," Jack said slowly, "that you have built up a theoretical picture of what you conceive the ether to be if it exists, and then derived properties from this theory and found out those properties don't exist."

"It amounts to the same thing, doesn't it?" Irwin asked. "The ether must have certain properties if it exists. Those properties will give rise to certain things in nature. If those things don't exist in nature the thing that must necessarily have those properties if it exists does not exist!"

"Quite logical," Jack said. "But full of holes. It all hinges on the phrase 'must necessarily have.' Let's call this ether your scientists proved did not exist a 'theoretical ether.' Actually there are an infinity of theoretical ethers—each with its own set of properties. Your scientists picked the first one they conceived and excluded the rest. They proved that one out of an infinite number of theoretical ethers does not exist. They immediately excluded the others from consideration."

"Perhaps," Irwin admitted. "I must concede that the science that built this ship works, and is far in advance of our own science. Undoubtedly you are right."

"Well, you may rest assured it will all be given to you," Jack said softly. "That's the reason for our coming home."

"You mean that Mars is to be given the secret of building space ships?" Irwin asked eagerly.

"NOT only space ships," Jack answered. "A million other things. You're going to get the basics of science. When you have them you'll wonder how you ever learned anything. You'll find that the velocity of light is greater in space than you think, the sun is over a million miles closer than you have measured it, that everything you still puzzle over in your science will be made known to you in ways that can be proven beyond any doubt. I don't know the state of your industry and science. Since you say that it is believed the ether doesn't exist, I can just about guess, though.

"Shortly I would like you to write a note to your people outside. You three must stay here during the quarantine period in case we have given you some disease that might cause an epidemic. In that note I want you to explain the reasons for your having to remain on board. Also I want you to tell them to bring history books and science books of all kinds so that we can form a comprehensive picture of the state of your civilization. Will you do that, Dr. Crabtree?

"Certainly," Dr. Crabtree said. A startled look appeared on his face. He glanced at his wristwatch.

"Oh," he groaned. "I had no idea that so much time had passed. Do you know that it has been five hours since we entered the ship? I wouldn't be surprised but what both planets are very much worried. It may even be that they have given up hope and believe we have been killed. They might attack the ship!"

As if in answer to Irwin's voiced fear an alarm gong sounded, and a sensation of quickly increasing weight made itself felt.

Immediately a loud speaker came. "They attacked us!" the loudspeaker said. "We're going up until this can be straightened out. Otherwise they might penetrate our shell."

"Let me at a radio," Irwin said. "I'll tell them we're all right."

Jack and the other eleven space men looked at one another guiltily.

"Sorry," Jack said, "You see, long ago our shell antenna was hit by an asteroid and sheered off. It would have cost at least one life to repair it in space so we decided not to until we reached a planet. There it would be simple to do it. So we don't have any radio."

"Oh," Irwin said dully. "Then what will we do? We thought the reason you didn't answer was because you were being secretive. It didn't occur to anyone that anyone with a space ship might not have their radio working."

"There's only one thing to do," Jack said. "By now Mars and Venus are convinced we are hostile, and that we have probably killed you if we aren't holding you prisoner. We'll have to go to the Earth. There we can repair our radio antenna and contact Mars or Venus and straighten things out. Also in that time we should know about diseases. Our original intention was to go to the Earth first anyway. We circled Mars because it wasn't out of the way. When we saw it was inhabited we decided to land. Now we'll just go on with our original plan."

YOU see," one of the other spacemen added, "We want to find out if the attempt to build underground cities was successful, and whether there are still people living there. There will be plenty of time to straighten out this misunderstanding while we are doing that."

"I doubt if it was successful," Irwin said. He told them of the flight to the Earth in a rocket ship, and of the printed material televised to Venus by the explorers before they died. He concluded with, "It is possible, of course, that in the stuff they didn't have time to send there is printing of later dates. However the material was not sorted chronologically, so the odds are against it. Another possibility is that the task of carving out underground cities went on even after the death of printing. If a substantial colony with the necessary boring equipment became entrenched safely in the underground, they might have survived. But for half a century after we contacted Venus both planets continually bombarded Earth with radio broadcasts without receiving any response, so it seems to me quite certain there is no life on Earth."

"Nevertheless we must make sure," Jack answered. And that seemed to be the consensus of opinion of all the space traveling unit of humanity.

THE day came when it was finally certain no diseases were carried by either the three Martians or by the space travelers that would be dangerous to the other. It was a day of gala celebration throughout the ship.

Irwin got to see the many details described by the reporter, Les Turner, in that series of articles in a daily paper so long ago. He also got to see the many achievements of the spacemen in their centuries of star traveling.

He saw a hydroponics section, a room fifty feet long, twenty feet wide, and twenty feet high, where more food was raised than a thousand acres of vegetable farms on Mars could produce.

He saw the smoothly functioning master controls of the ship in their ultimate perfection, and spent hours gazing through the ship telescopes at the stars, now so bright that the ten inch objective lenses set in the outer shell made possible magnification nearly equal to his own four hundred inch reflector.

He discovered that the people on the ship were all natural optimists, continually happy, and lived in complete harmony. He had difficulty telling them apart because they were all so nearly the same size at the same age, and were as alike in features as brothers and sisters.

In fact, he found that the space travelers told themselves apart more by peculiarities of facial expression than by shape of features. Of the several dozen men who looked exactly like Jack, only Jack had his particular way of smiling so that his eyes crinkled at the corners.

Jack seemed to have adopted the aged astronomer from Mars as his own protégé. They were together most of their waking hours and found more and more to bind them closely together.

They often entered into long discussions from which Irwin emerged with greater and greater understanding, not only of these star traveling people, but also of the nature of things. For example, one day Jack and Irwin were relaxed in the main salon. It was a huge auditorium-like space. In the exact center was a large fountain spraying into a pool. Surrounding the pool were exquisitely carved statues of maidens, in a rose tinted, semi-translucent stone—a rare jade. Over the vast expanse of the floor were artistically arranged flower beds.

Artificially induced breezes carried subtle variations of the perfumes so that at one moment the fragrance of a thousand roses would delight the senses, to be replaced in the next moment by the tang of carnations, or the intoxication of a million violets.

In another hour a concert was to begin. At the hundreds of tables for four that were distributed among the beds of flowers—all bolted strongly to the metal floor underneath the plastic surface, people were slowly gathering.

Jack and Irwin had come early, and were enjoying a cool drink with a strange, exhilarating flavor. There was a youthful light in Irwin's eyes that had been lost for a long time.

"I have a theory," Irwin said suddenly, "that I am dead and this is heaven. It hangs together, too. The mind tends to introduce understandable concepts in place of things coming to the senses of awareness that are beyond understanding. It is well known in psychology that a series of meaningless events are often retained by the memory as a series of ordinary incidents bearing little relation to the actuality. In life I was an astronomer. When I died and came here to heaven my mind immediately concocted a 'rational', though far fetched, sequence of incidents involving a space ship, stars, science, etc. to 'explain' and rationalize my being here. However, my mind cannot rationalize this garden of heaven. The obvious rationalization that it is the end product of thousands of years of devotion to beauty for all the senses of a fragment of the human race in its star travels is a little too steep. So my common sense dictates that I should find a more reasonable explanation for all this. The more reasonable one is that I am dead and this is heaven."

He glanced slyly at Jack and waited for the inevitable lengthy discussion of what he had said. He was not disappointed.

"Surprisingly enough," Jack said with perfect seriousness, "you are nearer the truth than you think. What IS reality?

What our senses bring to our minds is a PART of reality, but never any essential or adequate part of it. Our minds build theories on this inadequate collection of data from the Universe around us. The theories become the reality to the mind, while the vague, inadequate incoming impressions merely serve to excite into conscious awareness these memory pictures in the mind created by the mind itself.

"The mind is a very poor instrument at best. It's like a loudspeaker with very positive vibrations of its own. A quiet melody imposed on the loudspeaker by the reality of an electric current becomes distorted and lost as the natural tones of the loud speaker blare their cacophony over and over, as it is excited by the subtle harmony of the external stimuli. And that stimulus itself is at fault in the same way. Its overall effect is an illusion due to a defect in the receiving instrument, and only represents the thing that originated it in meager outline.

"Any 'reality' brought to the mind by the senses is a second hand, third hand, or even more remote representation of the reality which gave rise to it. In each of these translations of the 'message' originating in reality the same inadequacy and distortion takes place, so that what we see or hear is like an old wives' tale after it has made the rounds of the village a dozen times. All we can safely conclude from any sense impression is the stupid remark that where there's smoke there must be fire. In other words, we can safely conclude that there is reality. We cannot, however, discover the true nature of reality from a study of reality itself. That is the reason experimental science inevitably leads a race along the path to eventual extinction. The final symptoms are always unmistakable—a highly developed technology based on an almost completely erroneous set of theoretical conclusions. The theories themselves are unimportant. It is the fact that they are inadequate and incomplete and for the most part completely erroneous that makes possible the developments that bring disaster.

"A bacteriologist will confine a dangerous plague virus to a carefully guarded test tube and study it in an attempt to find an antitoxin for it. Later, if his civilization lasts that long, he will confine a synthetic virus just as carefully until he is sure it is harmless.

"A physicist, with his ignorance of the principle of life, with a vague understanding that vast power can be gleaned from a new source, and with the grandiose theories his mind has concocted from the meager facts of the event, will let loose atomic disintegration on a planet without concerning himself about its ultimate consequences.

"His fundamental modus operandi is to learn from experience. From the very essence of his method he dooms himself and his race to extinction when he finally does something with disastrous but not immediately obvious consequences."

YOU may be right in that last," Irwin said. "But I disagree with you that the data science gathers is incomplete and trivial, and that the more important data is missed. True, the senses bring very little directly. The microscope proves that about vision, as does the telescope. Instruments invented by the scientist replace the unreliable senses, registering data on paper as graphs, on photographic film, and in many other ways."

"Some," Jack interrupted. "I didn't attack the validity of experimental data, I merely questioned its adequacy. Let me put it this way, since you are an astronomer. Suppose you were to build an instrument that could measure exactly and give to you a completely true value for the magnitude of the force that drives Mars from its straight line path at every instant. From the data that instrument brings you continually could you find out the detailed structure of the solar system?"

"Of course not," Irwin replied. "It would be registering a resultant, not a series of details. Perhaps in time the existence of the sun and planets could be deduced from such data, but I doubt it."

"There you have it," Jack said, relaxing with a satisfied sigh. "Irresolvable resultants. I disagree with you that the structure of the solar system could not be built up from the data of the instrument we just invented. It could, provided that someone invented the theory that that data was a resultant, and the nature of the factors blended into that resultant. Then it could be proven by mathematics based on purely hypothetical basics that such and such a theoretical structure would give a resultant as a function of the time, and the calculated curve would coincide within one or two percent of accuracy with the actual data. But the existence of comets and asteroids would still be unprovable and UNNECESSARY, because they would add nothing to the accuracy of the theoretical conclusions. Only the details of theory necessary to the explaining of the resultant would be acceptable to science. The rest would be classed as fruitless theorizing.

"If two factors in a theory cancel exactly they are immediately excluded from the theory. That is a subconscious mechanism of the scientific mind. I know nothing yet of the state of theoretical science on Mars, Dr. Crabtree, but I assume it is much the same as that of the Earth back in the days before this space ship was built. Then it was believed and taught that when an electrostatic field was neutralized it ceased to exist. The OBVIOUS conclusion that a gravity field is a perfectly neutralized electrostatic field was not drawn. It was believed that electricity was positive and negative, or like and unlike. It was believed that all matter was built up from particles that seemed to be the nuclei of electric phenomena. Yet this duality of the basic particles of matter was not thought of in connection with gravitation and inertia, which were allied in the scientific mind. It was believed that inertial mass was of a single kind, and directly related to gravitation. It could not possibly have been inferred from the science of twentieth century Earth that the inertial mass of all the electrons in the sun was many times the total inertial mass of the sun; or that the gravitational field of the sun was an exactly neutralized duality of two electrostatic fields inconceivable greater than the residue effect called gravity."

JACK gave a cynical snort and then went on.

"In the, experimental method," he said, "if you have in actuality one force pushing an object in one direction with a billion tons pressure, and another force pulling at it with a billion tons and three ounces of pressure, you can concern yourself only with the three ounce resultant, and your theories to explain that three ounces must not introduce cancelable elements not immediately measurable and provable. So you prevent any adequate explanation of the phenomena you deal with."

"It's all very well for you to sneer at our science which has made possible my four hundred inch reflector telescope," Irwin said with some show of heat. "You were undoubtedly handed the true explanation of all the mysteries of the Universe complete in your elementary education. But you must admit that for any piece of data, granting that it is only a residue, and often a residue of things that are not in the least like the residue itself, doesn't that leave an infinity of cancelled opposites that could be introduced into any explanatory equation? If I were to say that one and one is two, you would immediately sneer at that and say that one and one is two million and two minus two million. I can't see that that would prove any more adequate than the simpler statement."

"Only if you were to insist that the second statement does not exist," Jack said. "There is a subterfuge in mathematics that I am sure you are familiar with, Dr. Crabtree. In a complex equation it is often possible to add and subtract some element not in the equation, and arrive at a very simple expression. The entire family of mathematical expressions equal to zero are contained implicitly in the unwritten zero added to every equation. They are there, and they may be written when it is necessary in some stage of manipulation of the equation."

"Well, what are you driving at?" Irwin said. "Are you trying to tell me that the experimental method will never uncover the nature of the reality of the Universe?"

"Exactly," Jack said. "Not only will it never arrive at the nature of reality, but inevitably in the natural development of experimental science, the theoretical science that grows out of it will automatically stalemate itself."

"Then tell me," Irwin asked, "How in tarnation did those ancestors of yours that discovered the true basics and built this ship arrive at them? If they didn't get them from the experimental method what did they do?"

"They invented a game called Theoretical Universes," Jack said. "You see, always before that men had made serious attempts to solve the nature of the universe. They made their attempt seriously, committed it to paper, and then died, and the inevitable end of their attempt was failure.

"It was like it might be if you were only allowed time to play one game of chess during your life, and you had to assert that your game was the true chess game. Or, more accurately, it was like it would be if you were allowed to play any game you wished, but had to finally settle on one game such as chess and assert that chess is the only true game, and the rules in chess are the basic, perfect rules that account for all games, and that all other games are really chess or they don't exist.

"Then these ancestors came along and decided that there must be an infinite number of games called theoretical universes, and the one played by experimental science was not the real one or the only one. They generalized rules to play the game. They said, "A game must have pieces, whether they are chess men cards or concepts. A game must have a set of rules. If you alter one rule or one piece you have a new game."

THEN they decided the Universe was a game. After that it was easy. They simply invented the science or art of inventing new games. After that they did nothing but invent games until they found one that did the same things on paper that Reality does to the phenomena that excite our senses and the needles of scientific instruments.

"Of course there are shortcuts they employed. They took what they called CLUES from the field of reality to act as signposts. Then they ignored reality until they had their game figured out. Their theoretical universe. When they could bring the theoretical universe to bear on the field of observable phenomena they compared.

"Actually it was quite simple. All the 'cards' could be bought at the local store, figuratively speaking. The same with all the rules. All they had to do was pick and sort and build and check. In a surprisingly short time they had it solved. Then experiment took its true place—not as an instrument of discovery, but as a quick check on the correctness of conclusions arrived at on paper."

"This was before this ship was built?" Irwin asked.

"Yes," Jack answered. "After the basic concepts that were to the theory what primal substance is to reality had been proven sufficiently so that it was certain they were not only correct, but also complete, their qualitative development went rapidly, with mathematical development following much slower. There was good reason for it to be much slower. Natural law as formulated by experimental science generally took simple form with the variables simply expressed. Constants covered a multitude of evils and all infinitesimals were dropped as not mattering very much.

"In the new work many of the equations expressing so called natural law, describing behavior in phenomena, were complex, with much of the hithertofore neglected phases coming into the picture.

"Light, which had been strongly asserted by the old science to be a universal constant, was proven to be quite variable. Due to its curvature in a gravitational field, which had been neglected, it was soon found to travel over a hundred and eighty-seven thousand miles per second in interplanetary space. We have found since then that this increases to over a hundred and ninety-one thousand miles per second in interstellar space. By calculation we know that in the heart of the sun this speed drops to a low of less than thirty thousand miles a second.

"Mass, which had been considered equivalent to gravity strength was found to have only an incidental relation to it. A billion tons of matter had more than a billion times as strong a gravity field as one ton of matter. Also, a ton of matter contained roughly nine tons of negative substance and ten tons of positive substance. The inertial mass of matter is always a residue.

"In rockets only this residue is used to produce thrust, and that at low velocities of the ejected mass. In this ship there is a separation of the two kinds of inertial mass, so that we receive nearly a hundred per cent efficient utilization of inertial mass, and with ejection velocities that are many times that produced in rocket blasts. Not only that, we gather our rocket fuel as we go along in the form of electrons, protons, positrons, and negative protons, separating them in magnetic sorters and giving them tremendous speeds in our betatron drive setup."

AT that moment the music began. The discussion was ended, as Irwin had learned from experience. These star travelers gave their undivided attention to music when it was played. And indeed it deserved it. There were subtleties of rhythm and melody and in mastery of expression that made the best Martian composition sound like the fumbling attempts of beginners.

And thus the days passed. Irwin lived almost a dream life. Whatever he wished to learn about in the morning was explained before he retired to his room in the evening. One day he expressed curiosity about a strange creature on display in a cage.

For the next few hours he listened to an explanation on the interaction of a living cell and its environment. Jack concluded this lengthy discourse with the words, "So you see that fundamentally each cell in an organism takes its food from its immediate environment and substitutes in its place the waste products of its metabolism. The food it gets is either the waste products of other cells or else food the other cells did not have time to assimilate. The total effect of the cell on environment is the diminution of certain substances and the increase of certain other substances.

"In the human body adrenalin is the waste product of certain cells and the food of certain other cells. The waste products of all the ductless glands in the body go into the environment, which is the blood stream, and then are distributed to the body where they form a very essential part of body and nerve cell environment. In turn, body and nerve cells give off waste products that are essential parts of the food of the ductless glands. They work together within certain limits."

Gradually Irwin's feeling toward these star traveling humans was changing. When he had first met them they seemed no different than ordinary Martians except in dress. Little by little the differences were appearing to his eyes. Their knowledge was based on permanently true basics rather than tentative theory. Their techniques were often too delicate and subtle for his comprehension. They dealt with things that scientists of Mars ignored as being irrelevant.

In one laboratory he saw technicians engaged in cell surgery, delicately cutting through the wall of a single cell and planting a foreign substance of almost molecular smallness, then closing up the wall again—all with remote control instruments, directed through a micro scanning device that projected the scene on a large screen in front of the technician.

In another section he saw machines making smaller machines, which in turn made micromachines that could be seen only under the microscope. He saw two way radios that fit snugly into the ear, slipping out of sight next to the drum. He saw robot calculators capable of solving the most complex of mathematical equations, yet which would slip easily into a vest pocket. He saw dozens of different machines with thousands of parts in them, which weighed a small fraction of an ounce when assembled.

And all this—the creation of super science and super techniques embodied in a fraction of an ounce of metal and plastics, the beings who did it walked quietly with unassuming friendliness; common men who might well have been walking along a sidewalk somewhere on Mars instead of living in a ship that had gone to the stars and returned.

THE Earth grew larger and larger as the days passed. It was their plan to go into the zero-gravity spot between the moon and the earth and make a survey before attempting to land. Already topographical features of the planet were visible in large areas, and these were being compared with maps on board to determine what changes had taken place and to acquaint the travelers with the locations of the ancient cities and countries.

The Martian space ship had landed near Oklahoma City on its ill-fated trip centuries ago. The star travelers planned to land at Chicago. There they would repair their shell antenna and establish contact with Mars and Venus and straighten out the misunderstanding. After that they planned to explore the whole globe and determine whether life could once again gain a foothold on the surface, and whether the ancients had succeeded in establishing themselves underground and still lived.

An air of excitement pervaded the ship as it began to decelerate to its resting point under the Moon. That huge orb swept majestically by as they used its attraction for a brake.

The shock recorder was registering an average of ten hits on the shell each minute from rocks ranging in mass from a fraction of a pound to nearly a ton. Yet so perfect was the shock mechanism that none of these hits could be felt in the central sphere, although most of them would have sunk a battleship in the days when the nations of Earth fought one another.

The television eye had been turned into the telescope, bringing the view of the Earth's surface to everyone on board. The telescope was directed by rotation of the ship itself, and in the routine piloting of the ship it was impossible to do more than get broad sweeps of the planet.

Each of the hundreds of viewscreens throughout the ship had its half dozen or so watchers, and the constant maneuvering swept every section of the Earth into view every minute or two; so it was impossible for at least some of those aboard to have missed the silver streaks with tails of fire that rose from the section designated on the maps as New Mexico.

They could be nothing but rocket ships, and excitement over them mounted rapidly. The obvious conclusions were drawn. The atmospheric radioactivity begun by the atom bombs so long ago must have finally died down. Since it had undoubtedly destroyed all life on the surface these rocket ships must be manned by the descendants of that part of humanity which had gone underground. Since they had not been in evidence when the ship from Mars had gone to Earth they must have returned to the surface only within the last century or two.

The question uppermost in the minds of all was, did those rocket ships contain welcoming or attacking details of men?

It would be twelve hours before the coming rocket ships would reach the ship. A general assembly was called to discuss the problem, and Dr. Crabtree was asked to give his ideas on the matter.

"I'm sure I would not dare to presume to more wisdom in the matter than you are capable of yourselves," he began modestly. "Yet from my point of view it seems that you must repair your radio at all costs. You are condemned without a hearing by Mars and Venus because of your silence. It seems you will meet the same problem on Earth. When those rocket vessels arrive they will probably signal you. Not receiving any reply they will assume it is because you are hostile and refuse to reply, just as Mars did."

WHEN Irwin sat down there was a deep silence in the assembly Finally Jack stood up beside Irwin.

"Dr. Crabtree is right," he said seriously. "We all realize what that means; death to at least one of us by the most horrible method conceivable. We have outlived the ancient doctrine of heroics. Nevertheless such a course must require a volunteer. I submit myself to the job, I not only have the qualifications necessary to repair the antenna, but also I have reached my full development and will lose little by death."

He stopped talking and stood silently, waiting the reaction to his words. Instantly a dozen others stood up. They shouted to drown out one another in their attempts to be heard.

Angrily Jack strode to the front of the auditorium and faced the gathering. He held up his hands for silence.

"You are a bunch of conceited fools," he said disgustedly. "You. Arturo, do you have the training to even recognize an antenna when you see it. Any of you, going out there and dying before your time, would be more trouble than the good you would do. Dead you would be a nuisance. Alive you would suffer."

"And aren't you being conceited in thinking that you alone possess the qualifications necessary for the job?" Arturo asked, his face red with anger. "Are you sure you could re-pair it alone and unaided? It seems to me you are a more conceited fool than I! Is it the service or the exalted position you would gain that attracts you?"

"Then you would join me and make the sacrifice on the possibility that I might need someone to hold a flashlight for me while I work?" Jack asked softly.

"Yes!" Arturo said after a moment's hesitation.

"Good," Jack said. "Then let's get started. There's not a moment to waste, because we don't know how long it will take us."

Jack caught Irwin's eye and smiled.

Two hours later Jack and Arturo were ready. Irwin had gone over the blueprints of the ship with them and the others who helped in the preparations. Equipment was loaded in the elevator sufficient to take care of whatever repairs were necessary, even to completely replacing the entire antenna equipment.

The two men were encased in space suits except for the helmets which were to be put on when they made their farewells.

Jack held out his hand to Irwin who took it, a tear in his eyes.

"Are you sure there isn't another way?" Irwin asked, his voice trembling. "Couldn't you build some kind of remote control robot to do the work while you stay inside?"

Jack shook his head.

"After the antenna is functioning again we could use a robot," he said. "But the outer shell is opaque to radio. There's no other way."

"But if you find the trouble and fix it in a hurry?" Irwin suggested.

"You saw the blueprints," Jack shrugged. "They showed you the details. It's one and eight tenths miles around the circumference of the shell. It'll take us hours to survey the job and determine what to do. So before we actually start repairs it will be too late to turn back."

Irwin gripped Jack's hand warmly. It was goodbye. Both knew that.

There was a final test of the radio equipment the two men carried so they could communicate with the interior of the ship after the antenna was repaired. Then the elevator door closed and Jack and Arturo began their slow journey to the opening in the outer shell.

As the door closed, blocking off their last view of the world they had known all their lives. Arturo turned to Jack and grinned.

"It looks like we talked ourselves into something," he said ruefully. "Think how nice it would have been to let somebody else be the hero."

JACK didn't answer, but bent over the packs of equipment and searched rapidly. He uncovered two boxes and ripped off the covers. Inside were two packs with straps dangling from them.

"Put one of these on," he said.

"What are they?" Arturo asked. Then his eyes widened in pleased surprise, "Parachutes!"

"That's right," Jack said with a crooked smile. "After we get the antenna in shape there's no reason we can't cut loose and drop to the Earth and spend our last days in further adventures. We can consider it our reward for our work."

"Hmm," Arturo said appreciatively, strapping on the chute.

Now both men put on their helmets. The elevator had left the shaft and was dropping slowly on the thin strand of cable. Already the air was growing thinner as the pumps sucked it into huge storage tanks in preparation to the opening of the outer hatch After the two had passed out and closed and sealed the hatch once more the air would be returned to the space inside the outer shell where it was needed to reinforce the cushioning effect of the shell, and absorb its share of cosmic rays that got past the shell shields.

When they stepped out of the elevator they made their last radio contact with the core and learned that the ship was now settled in the gravityless spot between the Earth and the Moon, and the telescope was following the progress of the fleet of rocket ships rising to meet them.

The hatch cover lifted soundlessly, revealing the intense brilliance of outer space. They hastily dropped filters over their eyes until vision was normal.

Already they could feel the tingle of the searing cosmic rays in their bodies. Each second hundreds of cells in their bodies were being killed and dozens of atoms were being blasted, to become radioactive centers of poison contaminating their bodies.

"We can't waste any time," Jack said into his head phone. "The less time we spend in space the longer we will live after we get away from the rays."

The two men separated and began a survey following their plans as they had been decided on beforehand. Each carried a pack of materials for repairing breaks. The rest of the equipment was anchored near the hatch, contact with the smooth metal of the shell being kept by board pads of sponge-like material impregnated with a tenacious, sticky material that resembled a non-drying glue in its action.

The same fluid enabled them to walk along the shell, being fed to the soles of their shoes through small tubes so that the normal exertion of walking broke the contact, but only a violent effort would break the contact of both feet and send them off into space.

Hour after hour they worked, pausing when they found a break in the antenna or a place where it touched the shell, then moving on slowly so as not to overlook any part that needed repairs.

At last they were done. They knew that capacity meters in the control room of the ship would notify those inside when the antenna was in working order. Then the powerful radio equipment would be connected and tried out. They stood well back from the repaired antenna and waited for that to happen.

A voice sounded in their ears.

"Can you hear us?" it said.

"Yes!" both Jack and Arturo shouted, their relief and gladness at having succeeded without calling for more help manifest in their voices.

"The rocket ship fleet is getting closer now," the voice said. "You'd better return to the hatch and get inside where we can take care of you."

"Nothing doing," Jack said, grinning at Arturo through his helmet. "We're breaking loose now and dropping to the Earth. We brought chutes with us."

There was a long silence. Finally the voice said, "O.K. If you make it we will see you on the Earth. Try to contact us by radio when you get down, will you?"

"We'll do that," Jack said. "Goodbye."

THEY joined themselves together with a hundred foot length of small but incredibly strong plastic cord and with a rapid jumping motion broke loose from the shell. Using what gas was left in their oxyhydrogen torch assembly for propulsion they started their journey earthward.

Then, by common consent, they fell asleep. It would be many hours before they reached the upper atmosphere. If they were struck by space debris they had no defense, nor had they had such protection since they left the interior of the ship. For interminable hours they had been working at top speed and their bodies had been receiving wound after wound from cosmic rays, which, though very small, set loose waste poisons that drugged their bodies and minds.

Their pilot chutes would open at the first indication of atmospheric resistance, pulling out the huge main parachute which, in the uppermost atmosphere, would slow their speed down to a few hundred miles per hour, and slow it more and more as the density of the atmosphere increased, so that when they reached the Earth's surface they would be falling only a few feet a second and land without harm.

Those in the ship picked up their receding bodies and followed them for several miles until they dwindled to mere points and were lost to view. Then they shifted the ship so that the telescope again dwelt on the approaching rocket ships.

A message was sent out over the radio. Then the set was switched to receiving and they awaited a reply. Finally it came.

"Who are you?" a curiously metallic voice asked haltingly.

"We are descendants of the people that left the Earth in this ship long ago," the radio operator said slowly and clearly. "Do you have any records of us so that you know of this ship?"

Twenty minutes went by before there was an answer.

"You are humans?" the metallic voice asked expressionlessly.

"Yes," was the answer.

"What a strange voice!" Dr. Crabtree said.

"Isn't it!" someone standing near him replied. "Doesn't sound a bit human."

The minutes passed and the rocket fleet drew ever closer, but no further communication came from the approaching ships.

When they were less than five hundred miles away a final message was sent by the star people.

"If you are receiving us peacefully please say so," the radio operator said. "Otherwise we will have to defend ourselves."

"How can you do that?" Dr. Crabtree asked his neighbor. "You don't have any kind of weapon."

The man smiled grimly.

"You'll see," he said.

The foremost of the rocket ships dived toward the star ship as he spoke. The viewscreen that brought the image from the telescope to all parts of the ship centered on this ship and enlarged it until it filled the screen.

A gasp of horror rose from every throat. The nose of the approaching ship seemed a mathematical point about which the front view of the projectile centered. Slightly off this center a transparent bulge could be seen, and inside this bulge crouched a figure.

THE figure was far from human. A bulging cranium topped two large, saucer-like groups of faceted eyes. Insect-like features completed the horror. Two thin arms could be seen manipulating the controls that guided the rocket ship in what now was known beyond doubt to be a hostile attack.

The ship and the face appeared nightmarishly for a second, then the rocket swung broadside. A pale glow spread over it.

The scene expanded to take in the other ships. The glow was spreading rapidly, and several of the ships collided with blinding flashes. The rest slowed, and then retreated in the screen.

"What happened?" Dr. Crabtree asked in amazement.

"We turned our electron stream on them," the man beside him explained. "It charged their ships so that they were repelled away from us. You know—like repels like. The surface of the ship throwing out electrons is charged with them. When the electrons reached the rockets they became charged too, and a tremendous repelling force was set up between them and us."

"Poor Jack," Irwin said sadly. "He will think Earth's inhabitants are human, and they aren't. How could such a race of insects be on the Earth? Where could they have come from without our knowing about it on Mars?"

PART THREE

Jack awoke, with the feeling that his neck had just been broken. Next came awareness of a soul-shattering steady shrieking accompanied by a slowly fluctuating, throbbing wail, as of lost souls in the deepest of hells. Then awareness encompassed a feeling of intolerable heat and crushing pressure.

He suffered these feelings without trying to solve their cause while his mind struggled into full wakefulness.

Then he opened his eyes.

At once a flood of memory returned. His first reaction was one of intense loneliness, kindled by the memory that there could be no returning to his home, the star ship, and fed by the bleakness of his surroundings in the upper stratosphere of the Earth through which he was now hurtling.

The jerk that had awakened him had been caused by the opening of his large parachute as the first thin traces of atmosphere caught at the pilot chute and dragged the large one from its pack.

The heat and tremendous pressure were due to his enormous speed through the thinnest of gasses—over eight hundred miles an hour, but rapidly lessening as the parachute acted as a brake, and the gas became increasingly more dense.

His body swung around so that the space-suited figure of his companion, Arturo, came into view. Relief bathed him like a cool spray. He was not alone in his misery, and come what might, he would have a life long friend at his side.

Arturo grinned through his transparent helmet and waved clumsily. Jack answered him. They looked downward toward the Earth. It spread over all the space below them, curving off at the edges. For the most part it seemed to be nothing more than a sea of whiteness mixed with dirty grey, but here and there the dark colors of land showed through, island-like.

The shrilling noise was growing lower and softer. Finally it died down altogether. A few minutes later all external sights were blotted out by a light frost that congealed on the outer surface of Jack's helmet.

"Hey, I'm blind," he heard Arturo shout good-naturedly.

He reached up with his hand and wiped off the frost to discover that it accumulated as fast as he could clear it away. After that he contented himself with a single swipe and a hurried glance at the enlarging landscape below until the warm lower atmosphere melted the frost away entirely.

There was no way of telling what part of the world they were going to land on until they actually landed. That time grew minutes away, then seconds away.

Below was a dense carpet of lush vegetation that seemed to spread uniformly to the horizon in all directions. Jack lifted his eyebrows when he saw this, for it was evidence of the end of the age of atmospheric radioactivity and the return of conditions that made life possible.

Absently he pulled on the thin cord that held him and Arturo together, drawing it toward him so that at the last moment he could release it and have plenty of slack.

Then a giant leaf twice as big across as his body rushed up to meet him. He felt the mild shock of its slap and plunged below it, to sprawl full length on a soft carpet of smaller plants, and dirt.

He climbed to his feet and turned to see how Arturo had fared, and grinned mischievously when he saw the space-suited figure of his companion swinging helplessly two feet off the ground, hung up by its parachute which had caught on the overhead foliage.

HE went over and gave Arturo a shove that made him swing in a long arc. The next time he tried it, Arturo managed to hang on to him. They fell together, laughing exultantly. They were safe!

"Should we test the atmosphere for dangerous germs?" Arturo asked.

"What's the difference," Jack said. "We don't have too long to live anyway. A few years at the most now, with our bodies burned by cosmic rays."

Arturo nodded. In a moment they had their helmets off, breathing in the strangely exhilarating atmosphere with its foreign odors of damp earth, rotting vegetation, and a thousand unidentifiable smells.

They gazed in awe at the giant plants and kicked at the sandy loam under their feet in puzzled wonder. The blueness of the sky and the whiteness of the billowy clouds were a fantasia of beauty that struck deep chords in their racial memory. Instinct told them they were Home!

Almost humbly they rescued their parachutes and returned them to their cases. Then they began walking. They had no way of telling direction, but with the aid of the sun they were able to keep going in a straight line.

They went a half a mile before they saw their first sign of moving life. It was a beetle as large as a dog—clumsy and frightened. It ambled away with its mandibles clicking in fright.

After awhile the ground began to rise to a gentle slope. Faintly a murmuring sound came to them. They followed the direction of the new sound and came to a river. It was about fifty feet across, its waters flowing swiftly and bouncing from huge boulders in a white froth.

After some hesitation they tasted it. In it was the smell of damp decay and the faint odors of fish and plant life that could be detected only because they were new and strange; but to the taste the water was sweet and satisfying.

They drank as if it were some new and delightful concoction from the culinary department of their star ship. They had not realized it before, but they were parched. Not a drop of water had passed their lips since they left their home in the central sphere of the ship to repair the antenna.

After drinking they laid down on the bank of the river to rest and enjoy the strange wonders about them. They were beginning to realize the lavishness of nature. Thousands of tons of water flowed past them every minute. Around them giant plants rose from the thick, rich loam. And now a strong breeze fanned at their faces and swayed the giant leaves of the plants. A rustling sound arose from the forest of vegetation they had passed through to reach the river.

Arturo fell asleep; Jack's mind was too full of speculation for sleep. They must keep on until they had found human habitation. They must try to contact the ship as soon as the Moon was visible.

The sun sank lower and lower toward the west. Another beetle stuck its head out of the forest and surveyed the two men silently for a time, then disappeared when Jack threw a pebble at it.

Jack fell asleep without realizing it. He awoke with the feeling that some loud sound had startled him. The sun was gone, but it was not yet dark.

He listened. Suddenly the sound of a feminine voice screaming came to his ears. He roused Arturo and told him to follow. Then he dashed off down stream in the direction from which the scream had come.

The river turned to the left. As Jack reached this turning, the river bank for a half a mile came into view.

A hundred yards away was a girl surrounded by half a dozen nightmarish creatures. As Jack looked one of these creatures made a rush at the girl. She drove it back with a blow from a stick held in her hand.

It was obvious that eventually the creatures would wear down her resistance. Jack hesitated and looked around for some kind of weapon. Arturo pulled up beside him.

Along the bank of the river were scattered rocks. Hastily Jack and Arturo picked up some about the size of a billiard ball and ran toward the girl.

She saw them and gave a glad cry. The creatures attacking her turned to meet this new threat.

Jack stopped ten feet from the nearest and threw a rock at it with all his strength. The rock met its large, bulging cranium-like head and there was a sickening sound. Then the creature toppled over, motionless.

The others turned and ran, their eight legs working with clocklike precision.

The girl pulled a short handled ax from its case attached to a belt around her waist and frantically hacked at the slim neck of the downed creature. The third frenzied blow severed the head, which rolled toward the river.

Jack suddenly decided he wanted a better look at these strange creatures and rescued the head at the water's edge.

The girl was looking from him to Arturo with saucer-like eyes. Their blue depths held an awe and wondering speculation.

Jack gazed at her in unconcealed admiration. Beautiful as were the girls on the star ship, they were colorless compared to this Earth girl.

Her golden hair hung over her shoulders and glistened with a life of its own. Her face and figure had the qualities which make the difference between technical perfection and genius. Her nostrils still quivered from the ordeal she had been through.

"You are strangers!" she suddenly exclaimed. "What kind of clothes are those you are wearing. They look like they might be space suits!"

"They are," Jack said, smiling. Then he frowned, "What kind of creature is that?" He nodded toward the decapitated head of the thing lying at his feet.

"They're the insect people," the girl said, shuddering, "There's so many of them that we humans are barely able to survive now. It won't be long until they figure out some way to exterminate us, and there is nothing we can do to prevent it."

"You mean they're intelligent?" Arturo asked incredulously. "That can't be. I've studied about insects. Their throat passes through their brain. When their brain mutates toward enlargement to the point where intelligence might be possible, it constricts their throat so that they are forced to become leeches. Then they live by not moving, and their potential intelligence never develops."

"Not any more," the girl said, shaking her head violently in emphasis. "About eight hundred years ago a new mutation took place that put their throats outside their brains."

SHE stepped to the head of the creature and with one expert blow, split it open. What she had just said became obvious. The bulbous cranium indeed housed a full sized brain with all its convolutions, and the throat passed under it unrestricted.

Jack and Arturo stared at the thing, beginning to realize the full implications of what they had learned.

"What kind of insect did this thing develop from?" Arturo asked.

"We don't know," the girl said simply. "The books say that insects were very adaptable, being able to change their body form and adapt it to many purposes. It may have sprung from the ant or the termite. It bears some resemblance to both and lives a communal existence as they did. But come. We had better get back to the cave before it gets dark."

She led the way downstream for another half mile, then turned inland. As they walked they got acquainted. The two men learned her name was Della, and that she and perhaps two hundred fellow tribes-people lived in a series of caves which opened not far away.

"I'm very much afraid of what will happen now," Della said, her lip trembling. "Those insect people that ran away will tell the others, and they will hunt us out as they have done to so many other tribes."

She walked faster and faster, and Jack and Arturo had difficulty in keeping up with her in their somewhat cumbersome space suits.

They came once more to the river which had circled around. Della led the way into the shallow water and went toward a place where the bank formed an overhang. Here close to the water level was a small opening. Della stooped and crept in this opening. Jack and Arturo followed.

After a few feet the tunnel heightened so that upright walking was possible. It was too dark to see.

Della took Jack's hand and led him. He found himself wishing he had taken off his space suit so that he could feel the touch of her hand on his, and decided that at the first opportunity he would remedy that error.

On impulse he lifted her hand and placed it against his cheek. Her soft laugh came out of the darkness ahead.

After several hundred feet she stopped. A moment later a section of the tunnel wall sunk back revealing a large opening through which light streamed. The tunnel itself went on ahead, so that unless one knew just where to look the secret opening would be missed.

On the other side of the opening was a large cavern. Perhaps two dozen people were there. When they saw Jack and Arturo they exclaimed in alarm and several men sprang forward. Della ordered them back and explained what had happened.

At once Jack and Arturo were dual centers of excited, growing crowds, demanding to learn more of the star ship and of the people who lived on Mars and Venus.

Della stood beside Jack protectively and finally insisted that an end be put to the questioning for the present.

"Here comes Gregor!" someone shouted.

The crowd parted. An incredibly old man was advancing, his white hair and flowing beard, together with his piercing blue eyes, marking him as a leader.

IN spite of his obvious age he walked with a firm stride and squared shoulders. His clothes were of the same dirty gray canvas cloth as were those of everyone else, yet on him they seemed different.

He stopped a few feet a way.

"They tell me you two men are from a space ship," he said. "Where is it?"

"Out toward the Moon," Jack answered. "We parachuted down."

In a few brief words Jack told about the space ship. Then he asked a question that had been uppermost in his mind since he had first entered the cavern and seen the gathered people.

"Are you descendants of the people who went underground when the atmosphere went radioactive?"

"Yes, the old man said sadly. "There aren't many of us left now. We've been fighting a losing battle with the insects."

"How did it happen?" Jack asked wonderingly.

"That we don't know," Gregor replied. "A few things are obvious. The insect people speak our language exclusively. They write our script as it has always been. They have rebuilt many of the surface cities and much of the industrial areas. So it is obvious that they did not go through a period of discovery, but merely adopted our civilization as it was abandoned by the surface people when they died out from the increasing radioactivity.

"We know that many kinds of insects went underground, living in sewers in the cities, in natural caverns, and in some cases in underground warrens they built themselves. We know from written history that the general trend of insect mutation was toward size rather than change of structure.

"When the mutation came that gave this species intelligence it also changed its bodily structure so much that it was never determined just what variety they did spring from. They had developed an enormous resistance to gamma radiation and long before we could safely return to surface life they had begun their struggle upward, mastering all that had been known at the End. When they discovered the underground cities and realized that the race that had created the civilization they had acquired still lived they began to systematically uncover these underground cities and exterminate us."

"But why couldn't you fight back?" Arturo asked impatiently.

Gregor shrugged hopelessly.

"In all the centuries of underground living we had forgotten how to fight," he said sadly. "I don't mean the technique of fighting. I mean we had forgotten the fighting spirit—the WILL to struggle. For so long each generation had been born into a perfect world where change was unheard of. Even now, dozens of generations after that paradise was taken from us, there are very few of us with the will to fight. We hide in holes, waiting for the final end. What is there to fight FOR? We number a few thousands at most in the world. The insect people number billions. Until you came we thought there were no more people any place in the universe than we few left on Earth."

"And now," someone wailed, "they know we are here because of Della's foolishness in going out, and they will find us and kill us all."

Jack turned to the man who said this. He was a big man, strong of build, with a godlike face and brow. In his arms was strength. Yet in his face was weakness and defeat—a weakness that had become the heritage of these people. The race of Man was not designed for a static life, and it had broken—grown morally soft.

Yet had it? The picture of Della facing the insect men and fighting them came before him. With eyes that were preternaturally aware Jack surveyed the faces around him. Suddenly he knew the answer. The women were not weak. Not all of them. It was the men. And it wasn't the men either. It was their tribe philosophy.

HE remembered incidents in his own childhood when he and his fellows had exhibited weaknesses. The weaknesses had been ridiculed out of them as fast as they manifested themselves.

That hadn't been done here. Here it was the weaknesses that had been nurtured by the attitude of the grown-ups. The philosophy of extinction rather than struggle, of hiding rather than giving battle. However justified the tactics of retreat may have been originally when the menace came, they were no longer a temporary expedient, but the living philosophy of these people.

Suddenly the full implications of this state of affairs hit him. He realized it could not have been humans that came up to meet the star ship in those rockets!

"Arturo!" Jack exclaimed. "We have to go outside and contact the ship and tell them the state of affairs on Earth."

"You can't do that," Gregor said quickly. "There is no place for us to retreat, and the insect people will be looking for this place now. If you go out you will further endanger the whole tribe."

"Do you think the insect people can't find you anyway?" Jack asked pityingly. "All they have to do is follow the scent of Della and the footprints of the three of us, and I don't doubt but what they have a keen sense of smell."

"You're wrong about that," Della spoke up. "After we came in, water from the river flowed down the tunnel and wiped out the last traces of scent. It they do anything they'll follow the tunnel all the way down and find nothing."

"And if you try to contact the ship by radio they'll find you," Gregor said.

"They already know where we are," Arturo said. "Those insects that got away are probably leading a party of them back here right now, and simple logic will tell them we can't have left this general area. They'll search until they find us. Maybe right this minute they have found the entrance to the tunnel, and they will KNOW we went in it, even though the river did wash away all traces of it."

"We've got to be ready for them," Jack said. "Quick! What do you have here in the way of weapons?"

"Nothing," Gregor said. "This was originally a storage section. No machines or source of power. It's lit by the cold light tubes built by our ancestors. We grow our food in hydroponic vats as we always have. Other than that we have nothing."

"A storage section?" Jack echoed. "What became of the stores?"

"They were cleaned out by the insect people long before we came here," Gregor answered.

"How did you come here?" Jack kept on.

"From the arterial channel," Gregor said. "But that is used by the insect people now. It would be suicide to open the place we came in at, because there are always insect people going along the arterial and they would see us."

A feeling of weariness overcame Jack. He had not realized what energy it took to walk through the soft loam with the handicap of terrestrial weight. A glance at Arturo told him that his companion was nearly out on his feet.

"Good old Arturo," he thought. "He would go through anything uncomplainingly. He would drop in his tracks still insisting he was as fresh as when he started."

HIS glance shifted to Della. How different she was than her fellow tribesmen. Her venturing forth onto the surface world for no other reason than adventure proved this difference.

Wordlessly he began taking off his space suit. Arturo followed suit, and soon they stood up, free of the cumbersome garments, dressed in their lightweight, colored shorts and jackets.

"You're tired," Della said. "I'll bet you're hungry, too."

Jack nodded.

He found that cooking was only something existing in ancient legend here. There were fruits and vegetables which outdid even those of the star ship in flavor—the heritage from the peak of the underground civilization, then peaceful though uncomfortable unconsciousness on the hard tile surface of the floor.

Although it was several hours later it seemed the next instant when Jack awakened to the gentle shaking of his shoulder. He opened his eyes without moving. Della was bending over him, a look of fear and alarm in her expression.

"Jack!" she was whispering.

When she saw him open his eyes she put a finger to her lips to signal silence. Then she bent forward and whispered in his ear.

"The insect people are in the tunnel. Any minute they may discover our hiding place."

Her frightened eyes looked into his questioningly. He could read there the faith that if anything could be done to forestall extinction he would do it—and something else that had nothing to do with danger and death.

He sat up and put his arms around her. For a second he hesitated, then their lips met.

"So this is what you do when I am asleep!" he heard Arturo exclaimed delightedly. Della pulled away in confusion.

"Go get a girl for yourself," Jack laughed.

"Oh, I have my eyes on one already," Arturo said. Then his face became serious. "Did I hear you say that the insect men were in the tunnel, Della?" he asked.

She nodded mutely, her face still flushed in embarrassment.

"What have we got that we could use for a weapon?" Arturo asked Jack.

"Nothing," Jack said crisply. "I doubt that anything would do any good anyway. Are you sure, Della, that there is no other way out of here and no other place you could all go?"

"There's another way out," Della said slowly, "But no other place to go that I know of."

"Where's this other exit?" Jack demanded. "What does it open onto?"

"It opens onto the other side of the hill," Della answered. "We never use it because if we did the insect people could find it from our spoor."

"Arturo and I will put on our space suits," Jack outlined hastily. "We'll go out that way and come around and plug up the entrance to the tunnel, trapping the insects inside. It's just a delaying action. Then we will radio the ship and see what can be done."

TWENTY minutes later Jack and Arturo peeked out from the concealment of the lush vegetation that grew almost to the bank of the river and looked carefully at the small opening to the tunnel they had entered before sundown. The first light of morning revealed the details of things with an unearthly clarity.

Almost overhead the moon looked down, its night brightness fading to a ghostly whiteness in the dawn light.

The tracks of many large creatures were in evidence in the soft earth proving they were in the tunnel, but none were in sight.

The two men wore their space suits once more, with helmets on. Incredibly tough, the suits would stop a rifle bullet and certainly would be impervious to the jaws of any insect.

In Jack's hand was a crude bomb made of chemicals from the hydroponics stores of nitrates in the cavern home of these Earth humans.

Jack and Arturo crept from their concealment and approached the bank of the river. They could see the dark entrance to the tunnel, and as they looked a faceted-eyed creature came rushing out.

It carried the struggling form of one of the cave men. Jack raised his arm to throw the bomb; then paused. Another, and then another insect creature followed the first, each carrying a human.

They ran in the opposite direction from Jack and Arturo and seemed not to have seen the two men.

"They've broken in!" Arturo gasped. "Throw the bomb! Stop them!"

"If I throw the bomb it will kill some of the people," Jack said desperately. He dropped the bomb unlighted and rushed forward.

He reached the mouth of the tunnel. An insect rushed out and met the full force of Jack's fist, backed by the weight of an armored glove. There was a sickening crunching sound as the insect's body case cracked under the blow. It dropped its human load and lurched blindly into the shallow waters of the river. Its antennae were vibrating rapidly as if calling out some warning of danger to its fellows.

As Arturo reached Jack to join him in the hand-to-hand fight, an avalanche of insects swarmed from the mouth of the tunnel.

The two men fought them off with piston-like blows, each blow connecting with telling force. A pile of squirming, dying giant insects grew around them until the creatures were leaping at the men from the mountain of their dead companions.

The end was inevitable. A wave of dark, angrily clicking insects swept over them. They felt their arms pulled back and tied together. Their transparent helmets became smeared with the syrupy blood of the things so that they could no longer see.

Then they were lifted and carried rapidly, helpless to know even which way they were going.

Jack cursed his helplessness. Yet in the heat of his self-condemnation and frustration realization began to dawn on him that there had been no attempt to kill him. Not only that, the captives from the cavern people had appeared to be unharmed.

COULD it be that the insect people captured humans and used them as slaves? A faint surge of hope grew in his breast. If that were the case it might be that instead of a practically extinct human race on Earth there was a large population of humans used as slaves by the insects. If that were so the case wasn't so hopeless.

He chuckled humorlessly. A simple matter of killing a few billion bugs who were as smart as people and perhaps could double their population every year, and who, on top of that, were almost as big as humans.

He was beginning to understand the hopelessness in the philosophy of the cavern people. Outnumbered, confronted with a constant reminder that their race did not have a monopoly on brains anymore, hunted from birth until death as their ancestors had hunted wild game, their mental makeup had taken its sad turn inevitably.

After almost an hour of travel at express train speed Jack felt his captors slow down and take several sharp turns. Then he was dropped unceremoniously to the ground.

The whitely translucent haze that covered his helmet was washed off. It was an eerie feeling to watch the face and forearms of a huge insect going through the intelligent actions of washing the helmet.

As his sight of the creature cleared he saw it in detail. Its eyes were a steel blue and gave the appearance of being a honeycomb. The hard face casing was a glistening brown, as of painted metal covered with a thin layer of oil.

Only inside the mouth was there a change from the robot-like appearance of the creature. There mobile flesh moved. A soft whitish throat could be seen when the creature opened its mouth. The tongue, brown with a bluish tinge to it, looked very much like a human tongue and moved in much the same manner.

After the insect had cleaned and wiped his helmet, it left. Jack looked around. He was lying on the ground in a large, fenced-in enclosure. Arturo was only a few feet away, and the bound figures of the cavern people were also lying near him.

He looked for Della with sinking heart. She was nowhere in sight. Had she been killed?

Gregor, the ancient chief of the humans, was lying not far away with his eyes closed and a look of utter resignation on his face. Anger stirred within Jack as his eyes settled on a small baby trussed like the grownups, its body contorted by its attempts to get free from its bonds, its face apoplectic from crying.

A gate to the enclosure opened and a procession of the insect people came in. One seemed to be some sort of a leader. His bulging cranium was nearly twice as large as that of the others, and his forearms were different, having dozens of fingerlike appendages.

He glided over to Jack on his eight legs and stopped, ordering another insect forward with a curt motion of his head.

The other expertly took off Jack's helmet, then stepped back.

Now for the first time Jack heard one of these creatures speak. His voice was loud and metallic—a deep base thrumming; yet it formed understandable words in English!

"You are from that ship out in space?" the creature asked.

"Yes," Jack said curtly.

THE insect studied him for several seconds silently. Then it spoke again.

"I am fully aware of your feeling of hostility toward us," it said. "In a way we share that feeling toward you. As thinking creatures we both believe we are the superior creation, and you with perhaps more grounds than we, since we have existed for only a few brief centuries while you have a heritage of thousands of years of written history and an unknown history before that as old as the planet."

Jack looked at the creature stonily, and made no comment.

"Ordinarily," the insect continued, "we do not bother with humans, but exterminate them wherever they are uncovered.

"However, we are very desirous of knowing how to construct a space ship such as that you came in, and are therefore willing to bargain with you to get that secret. You must know, since you know the potentialities of that ship, that we have been unable to effect its capture or destruction. In some way it is able to manipulate the forces of attraction and repulsion so that we can do nothing.

"Our offer to you is simple. Agree to teach us how to build such a ship and we will agree to segregate all humans in colonies where they may live in safety. In that way the human race on Earth will not become extinct, and they will no longer have to live in hiding. They will be protected and allowed to flourish. It time, when we and they get used to each other, perhaps the two races will develop a biracial civilization that will be ideal for both."

"And if I refuse?" Jack asked, curious as to why such a generous offer was being made.

"We have the science from which the details of that ship were contrived," the creature went on expressionlessly. "In time, now that we know such a ship exists, we can duplicate it successfully. We are willing to take a gamble and try what we believe to be truth serums on you in an attempt to learn the secret at once. Since your body chemistry is so different than ours that attempt will probably result in nothing but your death."

It was Jack's turn to be thoughtful. In his mind a plan was hastily forming. It might be possible to play on this hope of the insect people for the secret of the ship. He must learn more about them and report it to the ship. Then they could do what they wished with him. His life was forfeit anyway. He could guess why they wanted the ship. The Earth was too small for a race that could repopulate it twice over every year.

The insects had probably seen the signs of civilization on Mars and Venus—Venus which had once been covered with clouds, so the histories said, but which had cleared during the centuries just as the Earth was now clear of its radioactive atmospheric fires.

They wanted the secret of the ship so they could begin conquest of the solar system. In return for a possible amnesty on Earth they would exterminate the people on Mars and Venus! They would spread their empire to the stars!

THIS threat must be stopped, and it might very well be that if he and Arturo failed to do it or find a way to do it, it might succeed. The fate of the entire human race was more important than the fate of the race that remained on Earth.

Suddenly Jack smiled.

"I will have to think about this before I make my decision," he said disarmingly. "I can't think about it while I · am lying here, bound hand and foot; nor can I think favorably about it while my companion is bound, and all my fellow humans. Untie them and treat them decently. Allow me and my companion to be your guests, and show us a little of your civilization. As long as we know nothing about you we can't think favorably on your suggestion."

"Very well," the insect said. "I'll give you ten days to make up your mind. During, that time none of you will be harmed, and you and your companion will be my guests while I show you everything you wish to see. Then you must decide. If your decision is unfavorable we will use these people to find a truth serum that doesn't kill you. Then we will get the secret without your consent."

The insects untied Jack and Arturo first, then went on to the cavern people. The two star travelers stood silently, looking at each other with grim smiles on their faces. They each knew something which had not occurred to the insect man; something that was not known to anyone who did not belong to that small section of humanity which had lived generation after generation on the star ship as it traveled through the void: THEY COULD DIE BY THE SIMPLE ACT OF WILLING TO DIE.

They did not fear torture or truth serums. Nor did they fear poisons or any other thing. Body control, which became the proud accomplishment of a very few back in the days when the Earth was still untainted and covered by the races of man, was ingrained in these star travelers in their education.

Self-hypnosis was to them as ordinary as was swimming to the boy of the early twentieth century. Conscious control of the heart beat, even to the point of stopping the heart altogether, was part of their education.

As the cavern people rose to their feet after being untied, and chaffed their wrists to restore circulation, Jack looked around. Where could Della be? Had she eluded capture or had she been killed?

White haired Gregor approached Jack and said in a low voice, "I think she hid from them."

He had time for no more. The insect man, suspicious of their being together, moved closer.

"During this ten days," Jack said to the insect man, "I intend to return here every day to make sure you are living up to your word."

"I thought you would," the insect replied. "Shall we go now? I'm anxious to have you learn more about us. There is an old saying among your ancestors that in order to like a person you must know him. In spite of our utterly different body structure you will find that we are just as human as you are."

HE kept up a running string of chatter as he moved out of the enclosure with Jack and Arturo, surrounded by others of the insect race.

"As you know," he said, "when we evolved intelligence we found the remains of civilization already here. It took only a few generations to master the written language. We learned speech from the many prisoners we captured in the cavern cities we uncovered. We bred millions of special brains such as mine to unravel the secrets contained in the badly deteriorated books, and eventually learned how to restore them and reprint them.

"During all these years of mental emergence we have made startling discoveries which link us more closely to man than you would think. We find in the literature of the last days of mankind on the Earth that many believed that a new race would evolve. They of course thought it would be a mutation of the human race into a superior mental level. They thought that because of their belief that only the human race could possess intelligence.

"Among their beliefs was one that the human soul was immortal, and reincarnated, living successive lives on Earth. We have more than good grounds to believe that this was so, and that we too have souls, and that our souls once lived in the men that were here on Earth. It other words, the souls that incarnated in Man now incarnate in us. We are the final Race!"

* * *

Della watched the space-suited figures of Arturo and Jack disappear through the door to the outside, and helped get the door shut once more. Her heart was pounding with a mixture of emotions. She fought the impulse to run after Jack and face what ever might come by his side. She fought the fear that whispered she would never see him again.

She had utter confidence that whatever might happen, Jack would live through it. This conviction gave her a superhuman will to survive. If the insect people broke in they would probably slaughter everyone they found. Where could she hide? The hydroponic tanks! But she did not want to be alone. She would die of fright if she were alone. Who could she take into her confidence?

Arturo had looked at Stella the same way that Jack had looked at her. He had said nothing to indicate his feelings like Jack had. Yet Della felt sure that Arturo would be very pleased if she took Stella under her protection.

Stella was the same size as she, but with a rich auburn hair instead of her own golden color. She had always been a good sport.

Della found Stella after a short search and quickly outlined what she planned on doing. Stella fell in with the plan at once.

The hydroponic tank they chose was long and wide. It was occupied mostly by tomato vines which sent down very little root and provided a thick protection of foliage.

They slipped into the tank and swam underneath the plants for twenty feet, then let their heads rise above the surface. There, sitting on the bottom of the tank with their heads concealed in the thickness of the dense upper growth of the tomato plants, they heard the insect people break in and capture their friends and relatives and carry them away.

They were puzzled about this. They knew that ordinarily the insects killed without taking captives.

Della shrewdly surmised that the insect men who had escaped the day before had described Jack and Arturo, and the attackers had been given orders not to kill because the men from the star ship were wanted alive.

When the noise finally died away and the cavern became perfectly quiet, Della and Stella left their place of hiding.

WHAT should we do now?" Stella asked, unconsciously acknowledging the leadership of Della.

"If we follow them we'll be caught and then we won't be able to rescue them," Della mused.

"Rescue them?" Stella echoed wonderingly. "Are you crazy? They'll be dead before the sun goes down today!"

"I don't think so," Della answered. "Have you ever been in love, Stella?"

"Well, now," Stella blushed. "I think Arturo is awfully nice. But I doubt if he would even look at me."

Della remembered the way she had seen Arturo look at Stella and chuckled.

"He looked at you all right," she answered tolerantly. "This is what I mean. Maybe I'm wrong, but I have a certain conviction that Jack and Arturo didn't drop out of the sky and come into our lives just to be killed the next day by the insect people. I feel that you and I are going to live to be the mates of those two men, too. The way things look right now, it seems hopeless. We know that if we follow them we'll be captured. We've seen the insect city from a distance, and know we could not possibly get into it undetected, let alone search for our people and Jack and Arturo. I've been thinking of the sealed entrance into the caverns. It doesn't matter now whether the insects discover this place or not. Let's try going that way At least we don't KNOW we'll get caught that way."

The two girls crept warily through the rooms and corridors of what had been home to them since they were first born. At any corner an insect might be lurking.

Shortly they found themselves standing before the mysterious barrier to the underground. Although they had no way of knowing it, this place where they had lived had once been the underground built for the protection of the citizens of Oklahoma City in case of an atom bomb raid.

They were now standing before the entrance to the vast underground built secretly so long ago to house their ancestors; hidden from the knowledge of surface men lest they, in their terror of certain death from the radioactivity of the atmosphere, destroy the orderly retreat and destroy not only themselves but all those who had been chosen to sire the future descendants of the human race on Earth.

This secret portal was a large concrete square exactly like those next to it in the wall except for a symbol to distinguish it. This symbol and the secret of opening the portal was a secret handed down from generation to generation by the underground race.

Della and Stella knew that behind that symbol on the concrete wall was a buried mechanism that would activate in response to an ordered series of raps, pulling the block inward and then sliding it to one side.

If they started the mechanism and the door opened, they would be completely vulnerable to any insect that chanced to be near enough to see it open. Secrecy had not been built into the opposite side because it had been necessary only to prevent the surface people from discovering the underground cities, not to prevent the underground citizens of humanity from leaving.

Della hesitated only for a moment. To go the way the insect people had taken their friends would mean capture. To stay where they were would mean loneliness and despair. This was the only way left open.

So Della gave the series of raps taught her and all other humans, and the two girls waited breathlessly as the section of the wall slid away and began to move to one side. They peered through the first narrow crack with wide eyes as the sideward movement of the wall began to form an opening. To their relief there was no movement in the tunnel that they could see.

WHEN the opening had expanded enough for them to step through they leaped through, ready to dart back and run for their lives.

The tunnel stretched in a straight line running north and south. It was devoid of all movement. Where they had stepped through it widened into a parking area in which several cars were parked.

These cars were hemispherical with a flat base upon which rested seats which had been once beautifully upholstered, but which now were falling apart with age, the cushioning springs poking through the rotting fabric.

Rising from this circular platform which was perhaps eight feet in diameter was a plastic shell, hemispherical in contour, in which was set a single door of the same material with hinges and handle also of the same transparent substance.

The two girls had learned about these cars also. They knew enough about them so that in a few moments they were able to climb inside and get the thing going. A few experimental blunders that resulted only in mild bumps against the side walls of the tunnel enabled them to figure out how to run the car.

Pressing a green button on the panel in front of each seat (for the cars had control panels so that ANY passenger could operate it) raised the car mysteriously off the pavement so that it hovered motionlessly about six inches in the air.

A lever that slid in a slot on the panel regulated the speed, while a similar lever that slid sideways changed the direction of travel.

The bumps against the walls proved that the material out of which the car was built was still strong and elastic.

Della finally managed to get the car going moderately in the northward direction which would take them under the city of the insects where their people had been taken.

"We'll have to watch for exits," Della said as they slid along the tunnel. "Maybe we can find one that will lead right to where they are held captive. Then we could rescue our folks and Jack and Arturo and get away through this tunnel."

"I hope so," Stella said. "But I can't figure out why we haven't seen any of the insects. I always thought that they just swarmed all over in here."

"I know they used to," Della said slowly. The car was approaching a branch in the tunnel. "Be ready, Stella. We might have to shoot this car back the way we came."

She stopped the car even with the branch tunnel. It was much smaller. Barely large enough for the car to slip in. Twenty feet back it narrowed so that only a person on foot could continue. There was no sign of life of any kind.

"Let's explore this," Stella said. "I think it goes in the right direction."

She dropped the car to the floor and opened the door in the shell. The two girls stepped out. Ready to retreat at the first sign of movement ahead, they stole cautiously into the narrow passage.

Suddenly Della grabbed Stella's arm and stopped her. Then she pointed wordlessly to the wall. On it was the inscription denoting a secret opening.

Without hesitation she went through the rote of opening it. Instead of revealing another passageway the door opened into a small room.

Inured though the girls were to death and signs of death, they drew back instinctively.

THE walls of the room were lined with shelves filled with a thousand things they had never seen before—curious looking portable machines and instruments. In the center of the room was a workbench upon which a glittering array of glass tanks and tubes and glass-walled gadgets rested.

Also on the bench was what had once obviously been a man. A human being. One leg was gone at the knee and the other almost to the hip. There was a large gap in his abdomen and another in his side. His face was gone. And from each gaping wound grew a densely packed jungle of evilly red fungus. Its unholy stems glistened in moist redness. Each stem ended in a cluster of microscopically small white dots.

Yet this is not what had made the girls draw back and stop breathing in horror.

Glass tubing led from the array of tanks into one side of the figure. In the tubing coursed a bubbly fluid of yellowish transparency. Yet this was not what had made the girls draw back.

Impossibly, grotesquely, the chest of the thing that had once been a man slowly rose and fell in the rhythm of breathing. It is alive!

"It's alive!" Stella croaked hoarsely.

The two girls stood motionless, their eyes unable to break away from the horrible sight. And suddenly into their minds beat a telepathic voice, clear as a bell.

"Yes, I'm alive," it said. "I have stayed alive though it meant a living hell, waiting for the time someone of my own race would open this room and I could impart the results of my work."

The rhythmic motion of the chest continued without visible variation. The evil vampirish fungus glistened hungrily as though it contemplated attacking the flawless skin of the two girls.

"Close your eyes," the mental voice ordered.

It was almost impossible to do so, but finally the girls closed their eyes with a shuddering sigh.

"That's better," the voice said, "Now listen closely, because each moment of life is horrible torment to me, and for almost a century I have longed for this moment so that I could pass on my discovery and then die. Listen.

"When the insect race first broke into the caverns and began their slaughter several thousand of us who were highly trained in various branches of the study of life went off to ourselves—each to his own laboratory like this one, and began to work on the problem of defeating them. We all had different specialties and thus could attack the problem from every known angle. My specialty was cell genealogy— something that probably means nothing to you, for I see in your minds that the human race has lost its heritage and has now degenerated into small bands of people.

"One by one our cavern cities were discovered and wiped out by the insect hordes. Yet we scientists worked on, year after year. Finally we could no longer contact one another. We had to each carry on our work alone and without benefit of the others' experience.

"Before we scientists lost contact with one another we had decided upon the nature of the solution to the problem of destroying the insect race. Their mutation, we found, was not in the formation of the brain or its separation from the larynx, but in the activity of a certain gland.

"BY surgery we had determined that if this gland were destroyed in the pupa stage the insect creature did not develop intelligence but was just as his ancestors before the atomic age had been.

"My search was for a virus or germ that would attack this gland in the pupa stage. I won't go into the details of my work. It is sufficient that the details are written out in my lab book for anyone who has the ability to understand them.

"What is important right now is that on one of the shelves in this room are several bottles of virus I made that will ensure the downfall of the insect race. This virus is harmless to the human so long as he is not injured. If he is injured it sprouts from his wounds and becomes as you see me now.

"Find those bottles."

The voice stopped. Della opened her eyes and looked around, a new hope on her face. Something in the back of her mind—something not of her, seemed to be looking with her eyes. It seemed to whisper to her what each thing on the many shelves was. When her eyes came to rest on a shelf upon which were stacked several dozen small bottles of a transparent liquid she KNEW that they contained the virus.

"That is it," the voice resumed. "Now pull loose the tubes from the elixir tanks so that I can die."

Hesitantly, her mind seeming to struggle against every step forward, Della advanced to the bench. Her right hand reached out, the five delicate fingers trembling in indecision.

Her eyes turned to the horrible thing that had been a man. A great pity welled up in her blue eyes. With a sudden movement she reached out and jerked loose one of the tubes.

Slowly the sparkling fluid drained out to spread its stain across the dust on the table surface. After a time the rhythmic movement of the chest stopped.

As from a great distance a soft voice seemed to reach into her mind and thanked her.

With hands that shook Della and Stella gathered up as many of the bottles as they could carry. Then they left, not bothering to close the door after them.

Outside Della paused, then deliberately broke one of the bottles against the wall. Its liquid content splattered and soaked into the dry dust, Della knew about viruses and germs.

The narrow tunnel continued in the direction of the insect city, so Della and Stella followed it. Gradually a soft murmur of noise ahead grew louder and more distinct.

The tunnel took a sharp turn. Stella, in the lead, drew back suddenly and held her breath. Della advanced cautiously. The tunnel ended at a small platform overlooking a huge cavern.

The cavern was several thousand feet across and at least two hundred feet from floor to the highest part of the dome shaped ceiling. It had once been some sort of auditorium for the cavern humans, but had been transformed by the insects.

In the center was a giant monstrosity of living flesh. It towered nearly to the roof. Its bloated body was topped by a head that was almost entirely mouth.

A raised platform had been constructed, leading to this mouth, and an endless string of normal sized insects carried food which they dumped into the greedily working maw.

Far below on the floor of the cavern another endless string of insects were carrying away an equally continuous string of identical, sickly white eggs.

This, then, was the queen of the colony. Something no human had ever seen and returned to tell other humans.

The two girls, their eyes wide, stared breathlessly, their minds almost incapable of grasping the monstrousness of what their eyes brought to them.

Their vantage point was a hundred feet above the floor of the cavern. Where the side walls met the floor there were dozens of openings from which insects were streaming and into which they were carrying the white pupae, to be carried to other parts of the underground to be stored until they hatched.

The stream of insects from one of these openings stopped. A moment later an insect different than the rest emerged. Its head was several times larger than the common run.

Two human figures followed it. The girls sucked their breath in sharply. The humans were Jack and Arturo!

* * *

Jack and Arturo stared at the insect man who was their captor and guide with incredulous amazement. He continued talking, unconscious of the effect of his words.

"Perhaps not the final race," he corrected himself. "Perhaps in times to come there will be another race arise which we know nothing of now which will supplant us just as we have supplanted the human. Perhaps in a few thousands of years we will be convinced that no other race of creatures could be intelligent as the human race has been convinced of their superiority up till now.

"We discovered references to past races in some of the books we uncovered. They were mostly pictured as human in form, some giants, others even non-material. The human spirit was pictured as incarnating successively in members of each of those races. We learned of the techniques of remembering past incarnations and invariably when we followed these procedures we were able to remember when we were human."

"That interests me very much," Arturo said smoothly. "We have never heard of that before and, needless to say, it is quite startling to us. What is this procedure you use to remember past lives?"

"First of all," the insect man said, "You must keep uppermost in you; mind the desire to remember those past incarnations. In that way your mind will work toward that end. Then when you are asleep you will have dreams. Some of these dreams will be very vivid and have intense emotional feeling. These are the first awakenings of those memories. If you can capture some of them and place them in time you can say that you lived about such and such a period in a previous incarnation, and as a citizen of such and such a country. Then you must study all you can find concerning that time and its customs and ways of thinking.

"Little by little the memories will come, so that eventually you can say you were a definite person of that time."

"And you personally can remember former lives?" Jack asked, hiding his amusement.

"Of course," the insect said quickly.

"Are you sure it isn't self-delusion?" Arturo questioned.

"Hardly," the insect replied. If his voice had not been almost expressionless by nature Arturo could have sworn there was a note of contempt in it.

He opened his mouth for a hot reply, then saw the look of amusement of Jack's face and relaxed.

JACK had been paying little attention to the attempts of the insect man to convince them he was their brother in spirit but more advanced on the physical plane. After the first startled amazement at the idea he immediately recognized the probable explanation. Just as a man who is perfectly healthy can actually become physically ill if he becomes convinced he is ailing, so those who become convinced they can remember former lives by dwelling on them eventually can do so—especially if they study all about the period in history and the customs of the people they DECIDE their "memories" tie to...

He saw the simple, obvious truth; regardless of any truth that might possibly exist in the statements of the insect man, the FACTS were that he was human and this creature was not. HIS job was to find out all he could about the insect race and then get the information to the star ship. The insect race would have to be destroyed or it would eventually attempt to destroy the human race on not only the Earth where it had almost succeeded but also on Mars and Venus in a devastating Holy War.

So he let Arturo carry on the conversation and concentrated on the details of everything about them as they walked along.

The city followed the pattern of human cities as he has seen them in movies on the star ship. The buildings were probable authentic reproductions of those that had existed here before the atomic destruction so many centuries ago. The design was obviously not too well suited for the insect people. Therefore the inescapable conclusion was that they were imitative to a very high degree. Perhaps they lacked the inventive faculty. If that were so they would be easily beaten in the long run, just as the imitative Japanese had been in the Second World War.

Early in his youth Jack had read several books in the star ship library on insects. He recognized how the physical adaptiveness of the insect body was being used wherever possible.

The streets swarmed with the insect people. About one in every dozen or so had the large, bulging braincase. This type was obviously the ruling class—bred especially for their role. The rest had almost an infinite variety of special peculiarities designed for practical purposes.

One group was building a brick building. There was no scaffolding. Instead, each worker climbed up the brick face of the building wall. When he got to the spot where he was to lay the single brick he carried he would lick the spot, coating, it with some glistening fluid, then tamp the brick in place.

Then he would join the line of those descending for another brick. Insects with bulging craniums ran back and forth where the construction was in progress, directing the workers where to lay their bricks.

IT looked like nothing more than the busy, instinctive activity of bees in the hive or ants in their hills as shown in some of the ancient films on insect life on the Earth.

If it were not for the fact that this race of bugs had nearly wiped out the human race on Earth, and the bug walking at his side was speaking the human language and expounding theories that had required intelligence to create, Jack would have been inclined to doubt that intelligence played any part in this hive of activity.

He recalled pictures of warrior termites with huge mandibles walking imperiously about in the masses of smaller worker termites. All came from the same stock, but the warriors were fed differently.

He recalled that with bees, the drones, queens, and workers all came from the same eggs, but were given different foods which made them what they were.

Undoubtedly diet in the pupa stage made the difference in this race of insects also. Perhaps in some underground place there was a queen laying an egg every few seconds, and a vast place where the eggs were stored while they hatched.

She might or might not be also the directing brains of the colony—for that was all it was. An insect colony in spite of the intelligence and the reproduction of human cities.

In any case, destruction of the queen, if one existed, was the greatest blow possible against this single group.

Jack jerked his attention back to his surroundings. The insect man was leading them toward the entrance to the underground. This particular entrance had been made by the insects themselves, and was one of several similar ones.

An endless procession of workers went through this entrance and disappeared around a bend a hundred feet down the sloping shaft. Each of them was carrying three large sugar beets, thoroughly washed, but with the leafy top still intact.

A strange odor assailed the nostrils of the two men as they descended the sloping incline of the tunnel, following their insect companion. It grew stronger. It some way that seemed sinister and evil, it excited their emotions.

Jack felt it reach deeply into his subconscious, drawing, bringing to the surface racial instinct and racial memories dormant for thousands of generations.

Pictures rose against his will in his mind; pictures of primitive ancestors creeping into the dark privacy of the steaming jungle to mate with beasts and less than beasts and sire monstrosities in the lust rites of ancient devil worship. His nostrils quivered in the anticipation of something—he knew not what, and feared to imagine. His mind turned upon itself in disgust and loathing.

He drew back, and an insect behind him snapped at his heels, forcing him onward. There was no light here. He prayed for light to blot out the images that rose to his mind.

A picture more horrible than the others rose before him. A "memory" of lustful embrace, serpentine coils wrapped about him lovingly, caressingly; unblinking eyes of reptilian green holding his hypnotically; the slow, maddening rhythm of her swaying body causing his mind to reel in a delirium of ecstasy too intense for the mind to bear.

AND just beyond the range of consciousness the soft droning of the insect voice continued. What was it saying? It didn't matter. Nothing mattered. Ahead, somewhere, lay that which called to the very roots of his being—called with an invitation that could not be denied, yet which repelled with a loathing and revulsion which made Jack wish to kill himself rather than advance another step.

The Female embrace of the serpent changed subtly. The coils blurred into an unbroken surface of lecherous green and glistening, fungoid white. The caressing perfume of primeval slime enfolded him, seeped into his being, saturated his soul.

He retched in disgust at his own response, and the retching became an overpowering feeling of lust fulfillment.

Still the insect voice droned on, just beyond the borders of consciousness. He tried to grasp it and hang on.

A part of his mind seemed to stand apart and watch the rest. In it was amazement and wonder. What was taking place?

Abruptly the darkness ended and he emerged into a large cavern. He glanced at Arturo and saw beads of glistening sweat on his forehead. Then he became conscious of the fact that his whole body was bathed in perspiration.

Though the light had banished the mental images the exhilaration, the self loathing, and the insane ecstasy of every cell in his body was growing more intense.

A power reached into his mind and forced his eyes to look upward. He dimly perceived a huge, bloated body from the underside of which sausage shaped, white eggs were emerging in rapid succession.

His eyes seemed to have a will of their own as they continued slowly to rise. They came to rest far above on two huge eyes, motionless, metallic in their luster. Yet in those eyes was the soul of all things female, drawing, compelling... The Serpent lurked there, softly inviting. The unholy Lust of countless ages poured from those expressionless, honey-combed eyes in beams of intense, throbbing Joy. Woman was there, calling, inviting. Womankind of all past generations, collected and distilled until nothing but the pure Female principle remained.

Woman! Della. It WAS Della. How could he have been so blind! That was not some insect monstrosity. It was Della—gigantic, two hundred feet tall. She was there before him in all her unadorned loveliness, her arms held out invitingly, her red lips beckoning, her blue eyes caressing, her golden hair an ethereal halo about her head and resting on the white loveliness of her rounded shoulders.

With a racking sob of joy and relief he rushed forward to gather her into his arms.

In that same instant something flashed through the air above him. The illusion vanished.

For a split second he saw the real Della poised on a balcony set in the wall of the cavern. Then a surge of insects swept over him, bearing him to the floor.

"Della is here and in danger!" The words in his mind seemed to scream at him.

WITH a superhuman effort he rose to his knees, the weight of the insects trying to hold him down dragging at him. His space suit prevented their bone-hard mandibles from tearing his flesh.

With a sudden lurch he freed his arms and began lashing out with his fists. He felt and heard the sickening crunch as his fists hit home on creature after creature.

He had a brief flash of Arturo, his head flung back and a light of fierce joy in his eyes as he fought. Then he was too busy even to think.

His fighting improved rapidly. He found that these creatures weighed only about fifty pounds. Their heads were attached to their pipe-like necks by a loose ball and socket joint which pulled apart, decapitating them.

He settled down to seizing one insect after another by the head and swinging it around until its body pulled loose, falling into the forefront of the advancing horde.

It might have been minutes, hours, or days later. Passage of time had become a meaningless thing. Imperceptibly the attack of the insect horde began to change.

Where at first the insects advanced with clashing jaws and quivering antennae they now came forward slowly and seemed to freeze in a paralysis of fear as he reached for them.

Here and there insects were falling and lying still without having been touched.

Jack reached for the head of one that had stopped a few feet in front of him. As he reached he saw its eyes glaze in death.

He paused, swaying dizzily on his feet. His hand mopped the sweat out of his eyes and he looked around for more insects to kill.

The huge cavern was a shambles. Dead and dying insects in all stages of dismemberment were strewn about like some giant cataclysm had swept the floor.

Arturo had sunk to the floor, a nasty gash on his cheek. "Jack!"

It was Della's voice coming from the ledge where he had glimpsed her. He looked up. Then he grinned crookedly and waved at the two faces peering over the edge of the balcony a hundred feet up.

There were pegs set into the smooth wall leading up.

Jack went over to Arturo who was trying to stand up. He helped him over to the bottom peg and started him upward, climbing with him and cradling him to prevent him from falling.

At the top Della's and Stella's hands reached out and dragged the two men to safety.

Then Della was in Jack's arms, crying and laughing with relief. His bruised, bleeding hands cupped her face and drew it toward him. Then she was kissing him, her tears of gladness cooling his hot face like the waters of a cool spring.

The bloated body of the gigantic insect queen had not moved. There was a large hole in the center of her nearest eye where the bottle Della had thrown had crashed inward. And the strange, intense mental power no longer glowed from those eyes. She was dead.

Jack stared at the repulsive thing for a moment, then shuddered and turned his back on it.

"Let's get out of here," he said curtly.

CONCLUSION

IT was two weeks later. The girls had shown Jack and Arturo the crypt where the cave scientist had been found, and Jack had taken the laboratory notebook containing the secret of the virus.

From it he had deduced what had happened to the insects that died without anything touching them. The virus attacked a gland in the insect body which not only was the cause of their tremendous growth, but also was vital to their daily energy consumption.

Their deaths had technically been insulin shock. The virus had taken hold rapidly and was spreading over the Earth in an epidemic wave.

Della and Stella had led Jack and Arturo back the way they had come. In the hemispherical tunnel car Jack had dressed Arturo's wound, sterilizing it and sealing it, hoping it would not develop the same fungus growth that he had seen on the body of the cavern scientist.

Back on the surface he lost no time in contacting the star ship and building a huge fire to mark their location.

Assured that the ship had seen the fire and would land as quickly as possible, they had hidden, waiting for it. Ten hours later the ship had come.

With reinforcements Jack and Arturo had returned to the insect city to rescue the people held captive there. The streets of the city were strewn with dead insects. It had been a simple task to break open the gates of the enclosure and set the people free.

An aerial survey in the star ship showed that the epidemic was spreading fast and striking without warning. The insect menace would be gone in a matter of a few months at the rate the virus was spreading.

Dr. Crabtree had been one of the first from the star ship to set foot on Earth soil, overriding the vociferous objections of his two fellow Martians and the protests of the star people.

It was from his mouth that Jack heard the news of the straightening out of the misunderstanding of the Martians and Venusians concerning the star ship.

Two way voice-television contact had been established with both Mars and Venus, and continuous exchange of news and information was carried on.

Exhaustive tests had been conducted which proved that the atmospheric radioactivity of the Earth's atmosphere had dropped well below the danger level. C-14 content was still high and would shorten the life span of humans for thousands of years to come, but a normal life span of nearly a century could be expected and records proved that it would exceed the life span of their ancestors who had been thick on the surface so many centuries before.

Plans were already under way for recolonization of the Earth and exploration of the subterranean cities as well as rehabilitation of the wandering tribes of earth people whenever they could be found.

THOUSANDS of Venusians and Martians were clamoring for the opportunity to come to the Earth and colonize. Plans for construction of more of the star ships were being laid by the Martian and Venusian governments and their foundries were at work learning the process of making the stainless steel so vital to the construction of the ship.

Jack and Della sat on a rock near the bank of the river where they had first met. The sun had dropped beneath the horizon at their backs unnoticed by them, and now the stars were coming out, one by one.

The moon, already half way toward the zenith, looked down on them benignly from behind the scudding clouds. The bull fiddle strumming of a giant cricket came from far away, and over the tops of the forest growth could be seen the upper part of the star ship, like a second moon, where it rested at anchor just outside the insect city.

The two sat side by side, his arm about her waist, their forms blended into one in the darkness as it grew deeper with the coming of night.

Wordlessly he brushed his lips against her cheek.

"Just think, darling," he said softly, "for the rest of our lives we can come here, just us two, and watch the stars."

"You're sure you don't want to go up there?" Della asked hesitantly. "After all, that's your home—out there where the stars are."

Jack laughed briefly.

"Not a chance of it," he reassured her. "It can't compare with a sunset, or the blue sky of Earth, or the feel of a cool breeze and the realization that that breeze came from a thousand miles away, drifting under a topless roof of space.

"I made my choice centuries ago, it seems now, when Arturo and I went out to fix the radio antenna of the ship. In that brief time so many millions of atoms in our bodies changed their coats that we could not have returned to the interior of the ship if we had wished. It would have meant pollution of the rest."

"But here it doesn't matter. We're polluted already," Della laughed.

"That's right," Jack said. "But polluted or not, I love you, Della. Let's build a home right here on this spot where I first saw you."

"Right here," Della agreed. "But what of your friends on the star ship? Are they going to stay there? It would be so nice if they could join the rest of us and settle down here."

"They've about decided to settle on Venus," Jack answered. "Venus went through the same thing the Earth did long ago and is quite free from radioactive contamination now. There they will supervise the building of more and more star ships. Some of those may go out where we did and colonize some of the planets we found that are able to support human life. Someday maybe the whole galaxy will be dotted with Earths like this one, with billions of human beings on them. Maybe our great-great-great-great grandchildren will be among those who settle on the planets out among the stars."

"Are there other peoples out there?" Della asked.

"I don't know," Jack said slowly. "You might say our whole voyage was like it would be if you stuck your head in just one of the tunnels near here and then were asked to decide if there were people on the Earth. There is so much space. And there were so many things we couldn't explain about our voyage. There are dark planets drifting in the void between here and the nearest star which could have millions of people living down under the surface where it wouldn't take much to keep it warm.

"Sometimes we were almost convinced that some of them were inhabited, but the gravity at their surface was too great to run the risk of finding out.

"The universe is a strange place, and full of many strange things. But most beautiful of them all is the Earth, and the most beautiful thing on Earth is a girl by the name of Della."

With a sigh of contentment Della snuggled closer and laid her head on Jack's shoulder; and above, the stars looked down, twinkling, while from afar off came the muted sound of the cricket, strumming his bull fiddle note.

THE END

If you've enjoyed this book, you will not want to miss these terrific titles…

ARMCHAIR SCI-FI & HORROR DOUBLE NOVELS, $12.95 each

D-1   **THE GALAXY RAIDERS** by William P. McGivern
         SPACE STATION #1 by Frank Belknap Long

D-2   **THE PROGRAMMED PEOPLE** by Jack Sharkey
         SLAVES OF THE CRYSTAL BRAIN by William Carter Sawtelle

D-3   **YOU'RE ALL ALONE** by Fritz Leiber
         THE LIQUID MAN by Bernard C. Gilford

D-4   **CITADEL OF THE STAR LORDS** by Edmund Hamilton
         VOYAGE TO ETERNITY by Milton Lesser

D-5   **IRON MEN OF VENUS** by Don Wilcox
         THE MAN WITH ABSOLUTE MOTION by Noel Loomis

D-6   **WHO SOWS THE WIND...** by Rog Phillips
         THE PUZZLE PLANET by Robert A. W. Lowndes

D-7   **PLANET OF DREAD** by Murray Leinster
         TWICE UPON A TIME by Charles L. Fontenay

D-8   **THE TERROR OUT OF SPACE** by Dwight V. Swain
         QUEST OF THE GOLDEN APE by Ivar Jorgensen and Adam Chase

D-9   **SECRET OF MARRACOTT DEEP** by Henry Slesar
         PAWN OF THE BLACK FLEET by Mark Clifton.

D-10   **BEYOND THE RINGS OF SATURN** by Robert Moore Williams
         A MAN OBSESSED by Alan E. Nourse

ARMCHAIR SCIENCE FICTION CLASSICS, $12.95 each

C-1   **THE GREEN MAN**
         by Harold M. Sherman

C-2   **A TRACE OF MEMORY**
         By Keith Laumer

C-3   **INTO PLUTONIAN DEPTHS**
         by Stanton A. Coblentz

ARMCHAIR MASTERS OF SCIENCE FICTION SERIES, $16.95 each

M-1   **MASTERS OF SCIENCE FICTION, Vol. One**
         Bryce Walton—"Dark of the Moon" and other tales

M-2   **MASTERS OF SCIENCE FICTION, Vol. Two**
         Jerome Bixby—"One Way Street" and other tales

If you've enjoyed this book, you will not want to miss these terrific titles…

ARMCHAIR SCI-FI & HORROR DOUBLE NOVELS, $12.95 each

D-11   **PERIL OF THE STARMEN** by Kris Neville
       THE STRANGE INVASION by Murray Leinster

D-12   **THE STAR LORD** by Boyd Ellanby
       CAPTIVES OF THE FLAME by Samuel R. Delany

D-13   **MEN OF THE MORNING STAR** by Edmund Hamilton
       PLANET FOR PLUNDER by Hal Clement and Sam Merwin, Jr.

D-14   **ICE CITY OF THE GORGON** by Chester S. Geier and Richard Shaver
       WHEN THE WORLD TOTTERED by Lester Del Rey

D-15   **WORLDS WITHOUT END** by Clifford D. Simak
       THE LAVENDER VINE OF DEATH by Don Wilcox

D-16   **SHADOW ON THE MOON** by Joe Gibson
       ARMAGEDDON EARTH by Geoff St. Reynard

D-17   **THE GIRL WHO LOVED DEATH** by Paul W. Fairman
       SLAVE PLANET by Laurence M. Janifer

D-18   **SECOND CHANCE** by J. F. Bone
       MISSION TO A DISTANT STAR by Frank Belknap Long

D-19   **THE SYNDIC** by C. M. Kornbluth
       FLIGHT TO FOREVER by Poul Anderson

D-20   **SOMEWHERE I'LL FIND YOU** by Milton Lesser
       THE TIME ARMADA by Fox B. Holden

ARMCHAIR SCIENCE FICTION CLASSICS, $12.95 each

C-4   **CORPUS EARTHLING**
       by Louis Charbonneau

C-5   **THE TIME DISSOLVER**
       by Jerry Sohl

C-6   **WEST OF THE SUN**
       by Edgar Pangborn

ARMCHAIR SCIENCE FICTION & HORROR GEMS SERIES, $12.95 each

G-1   **SCIENCE FICTION GEMS, Vol. One**
       Isaac Asimov and others

G-2   **HORROR GEMS, Vol. One**
       Carl Jacobi and others

If you've enjoyed this book, you will not want to miss these terrific titles…

ARMCHAIR SCI-FI & HORROR DOUBLE NOVELS, $12.95 each

D-21 **EMPIRE OF EVIL** by Robert Arnette
THE SIGN OF THE TIGER by Alan E. Nourse & J. A. Meyer

D-22 **OPERATION SQUARE PEG** by Frank Belknap Long
ENCHANTRESS OF VENUS by Leigh Brackett

D-23 **THE LIFE WATCH** by Lester Del Rey
CREATURES OF THE ABYSS by Murray Leinster

D-24 **LEGION OF LAZARUS** by Edmond Hamilton
STAR HUNTER by Andre Norton

D-25 **EMPIRE OF WOMEN** by John Fletcher
ONE OF OUR CITIES IS MISSING by Irving Cox

D-26 **THE WRONG SIDE OF PARADISE** by Raymond F. Jones
THE INVOLUNTARY IMMORTALS by Rog Phillips

D-27 **EARTH QUARTER** by Damon Knight
ENVOY TO NEW WORLDS by Keith Laumer

D-28 **SLAVES TO THE METAL HORDE** by Milton Lesser
HUNTERS OUT OF TIME by Joseph E. Kelleam

D-29 **RX JUPITER SAVE US** by Ward Moore
BEWARE THE USURPERS by Geoff St. Reynard

D-30 **SECRET OF THE SERPENT** by Don Wilcox
CRUSADE ACROSS THE VOID by Dwight V. Swain

ARMCHAIR SCIENCE FICTION CLASSICS, $12.95 each

C-7 **THE SHAVER MYSTERY, Book One**
by Richard S. Shaver

C-8 **THE SHAVER MYSTERY, Book Two**
by Richard S. Shaver

C-9 **MURDER IN SPACE**
by David V. Reed

ARMCHAIR MASTERS OF SCIENCE FICTION SERIES, $16.95 each

M-3 **MASTERS OF SCIENCE FICTION, Vol. Three**
Robert Sheckley, "The Perfect Woman" and other tales

M-4 **MASTERS OF SCIENCE FICTION, Vol. Four**
Mack Reynolds, Part One, "Stowaway" and other tales

If you've enjoyed this book, you will not want to miss these terrific titles…

ARMCHAIR SCI-FI & HORROR DOUBLE NOVELS, $12.95 each

D-31   **A HOAX IN TIME** by Keith Laumer
INSIDE EARTH by Poul Anderson

D-32   **TERROR STATION** by Dwight V. Swain
THE WEAPON FROM ETERNITY by Dwight V. Swain

D-33   **THE SHIP FROM INFINITY** by Edmond Hamilton
TAKEOFF by C. M. Kornbluth

D-34   **THE METAL DOOM** by David H. Keller
TWELVE TIMES ZERO by Howard Browne

D-35   **HUNTERS OUT OF SPACE** by Joseph Kelleam
INVASION FROM THE DEEP by Paul W. Fairman,

D-36   **THE BEES OF DEATH** by Robert Moore Williams
A PLAGUE OF PYTHONS by Frederick Pohl

D-37   **THE LORDS OF QUARMALL** by Fritz Leiber and Harry Fischer
BEACON TO ELSEWHERE by James H. Schmitz

D-38   **BEYOND PLUTO** by John S. Campbell
ARTERY OF FIRE by Thomas N. Scortia

D-39   **SPECIAL DELIVERY** by Kris Neville
NO TIME FOR TOFFEE by Charles F. Meyers

D-40   **JUNGLE IN THE SKY** by Milton Lesser
RECALLED TO LIFE by Robert Silverberg

ARMCHAIR SCIENCE FICTION CLASSICS, $12.95 each

C-10   **MARS IS MY DESTINATION**
by Frank Belknap Long

C-12   **SO SHALL YE REAP**
by Rog Phillips

C-11   **SPACE PLAGUE**
by George O. Smith

ARMCHAIR SCIENCE FICTION & HORROR GEMS SERIES, $12.95 each

G-3   **SCIENCE FICTION GEMS, Vol. Two**
James Blish and others

G-4   **HORROR GEMS, Vol. Two**
Joseph Payne Brennan and others

If you've enjoyed this book, you will not want to miss these terrific titles…

ARMCHAIR SCI-FI & HORROR DOUBLE NOVELS, $12.95 each

D-61 **THE MAN WHO STOPPED AT NOTHING** by Paul W. Fairman
TEN FROM INFINITY by Ivar Jorgensen

D-62 **WORLDS WITHIN** by Rog Phillips
THE SLAVE by C.M. Kornbluth

D-63 **SECRET OF THE BLACK PLANET** by Milton Lesser
THE OUTCASTS OF SOLAR III by Emmett McDowell

D-64 **WEB OF THE WORLDS** by Harry Harrison and Katherine MacLean
RULE GOLDEN by Damon Knight

D-65 **TEN TO THE STARS** by Raymond Z. Gallun
THE CONQUERORS by David H. Keller, M. D.

D-66 **THE HORDE FROM INFINITY** by Dwight V. Swain
THE DAY THE EARTH FROZE by Gerald Hatch

D-67 **THE WAR OF THE WORLDS** by H. G. Wells
THE TIME MACHINE by H. G. Wells

D-68 **STARCOMBERS** by Edmond Hamilton
THE YEAR WHEN STARDUST FELL by Raymond F. Jones

D-69 **HOCUS-POCUS UNIVERSE** by Jack Williamson
QUEEN OF THE PANTHER WORLD by Berkeley Livingston

D-70 **BATTERING RAMS OF SPACE** by Don Wilcox
DOOMSDAY WING by George H. Smith

ARMCHAIR SCIENCE FICTION & FANTASY CLASSICS, $12.95 each

C-19 **EMPIRE OF JEGGA**
by David V. Reed

C-20 **THE TOMORROW PEOPLE**
by Judith Merril

C-21 **THE MAN FROM YESTERDAY**
by Howard Browne as by Lee Francis

C-22 **THE TIME TRADERS**
by Andre Norton

C-23 **ISLANDS OF SPACE**
by John W. Campbell

C-24 **THE GALAXY PRIMES**
by E. E. "Doc" Smith

If you've enjoyed this book, you will not want to miss these terrific titles…

ARMCHAIR SCI-FI & HORROR DOUBLE NOVELS, $12.95 each

D-71   **THE DEEP END** by Gregory Luce
TO WATCH BY NIGHT by Robert Moore Williams

D-72   **SWORDSMAN OF LOST TERRA** by Poul Anderson
PLANET OF GHOSTS by David V. Reed

D-73   **MOON OF BATTLE** by J. J. Allerton
THE MUTANT WEAPON by Murray Leinster

D-74   **OLD SPACEMEN NEVER DIE!** John Jakes
RETURN TO EARTH by Bryan Berry

D-75   **THE THING FROM UNDERNEATH** by Milton Lesser
OPERATION INTERSTELLAR by George O. Smith

D-76   **THE BURNING WORLD** by Algis Budrys
FOREVER IS TOO LONG by Chester S. Geier

D-77   **THE COSMIC JUNKMAN** by Rog Phillips
THE ULTIMATE WEAPON by John W. Campbell

D-78   **THE TIES OF EARTH** by James H. Schmitz
CUE FOR QUIET by Thomas L. Sherred

D-79   **SECRET OF THE MARTIANS** by Paul W. Fairman
THE VARIABLE MAN by Philip K. Dick

D-80   **THE GREEN GIRL** by Jack Williamson
THE ROBOT PERIL by Don Wilcox

ARMCHAIR SCIENCE FICTION CLASSICS, $12.95 each

C-25   **THE STAR KINGS**
by Edmond Hamilton

C-26   **NOT IN SOLITUDE**
by Kenneth Gantz

C-32   **PROMETHEUS II**
by S. J. Byrne

ARMCHAIR SCIENCE FICTION & HORROR GEMS SERIES, $12.95 each

G-7   **SCIENCE FICTION GEMS, Vol. Seven**
Jack Sharkey and others

G-8   **HORROR GEMS, Vol. Eight**
Seabury Quinn and others

If you've enjoyed this book, you will not want to miss these terrific titles…

ARMCHAIR SCI-FI & HORROR DOUBLE NOVELS, $12.95 each

D-81   **THE LAST PLEA** by Robert Bloch
        OMEGA by Robert Sheckley

D-82   **WOMAN FROM ANOTHER PLANET** by Frank Belknap Long
        HOMECALLING by Judith Merril

D-83   **WHEN TWO WORLDS MEET** by Robert Moore Williams
        THE MAN WHO HAD NO BRAINS by Jeff Sutton

D-84   **THE SPECTRE OF SUICIDE SWAMP** by E. K. Jarvis
        IT'S MAGIC, YOU DOPE! by Jack Sharkey

D-85   **THE STARSHIP FROM SIRIUS** by Rog Phillips
        FINAL WEAPON by Everett Cole

D-86   **TREASURE ON THUNDER MOON** by Edmond Hamilton
        TRAIL OF THE ASTROGAR by Henry Haase

D-87   **THE VENUS ENIGMA** by Joe Gibson
        THE WOMAN IN SKIN 13 by Paul W. Fairman

D-88   **THE MAD ROBOT** by William P. McGivern
        THE RUNNING MAN by J. Holly Hunter

D-89   **VENGEANCE OF KYVOR** by Randall Garrett
        AT THE EARTH'S CORE by Edgar Rice Burroughs

D-90   **DWELLERS OF THE DEEP** by Don Wilcox
        NIGHT OF THE LONG KNIVES by Fritz Leiber

ARMCHAIR SCIENCE FICTION CLASSICS, $12.95 each

C-28   **THE MAN FROM TOMORROW**
        by Stanton A. Cobllentz

C-29   **THE GREEN MAN OF GRAYPEC**
        by Festus Pragnell

C-30   **THE SHAVER MYSTERY, Book Four**
        by Richard S. Shaver

ARMCHAIR MASTERS OF SCIENCE FICTION SERIES, $16.95 each

MS-7   **MASTERS OF SCIENCE FICTION AND FANTASY, Vol. Seven**
        Lester del Rey, "The Band Played On" and other tales

MS-8   **MASTERS OF SCIENCE FICTION, Vol. Eight**
        Milton Lesser, "'A' is for Android" and other tales

THE NEW WEAPON OF CHOICE...

Throughout human history, Man has developed (and used) many deadly weapons of all shapes and sizes—from the crude stone knives of prehistoric days, to the muskets of revolutionary times, to the terrifying multi-megaton nuclear bombs of today. But here, in the not too distant future, the weapon that was the most effective in destroying a man's hopes and security was…the file folder. That was the weapon Howard Morely truly loved and knew how to use best. But there was something far more potent to come.

Join veteran science fiction author Everett B. Cole as he spins an engaging tale of a grim future, where telepathy machines exist and the world is run by strict military rules.

CAST OF CHARACTERS

HOWARD MORELY
He was a District Director who felt superior to most others in this class-ridden society of the future.   He was in for a big surprise.

PAUL GRAHAM
A new telepathy device was his baby, and naturally, the government took it—now what would happen to the world?

HAROLD BOND
He was a Sector Leader, which was better than most jobs, but things were very taut when it came to working for Morely.

ELAINE GRAHAM
She was fearful for her husband and family. With Sector Leaders always checking and accusing, though, anything could happen!

WARD KIRK
He found out—the hard way— that the old lesson about keeping your mouth shut also applied to thinking!

GEORGE HARWOOD
An easy-going District Director who was liked by most of his constituents, but whom Morely was incredibly jealous of.

DEVORE
Morely asked him to do something very illegal, but he came up with his own solution…

FINAL WEAPON

By
EVERETT B. COLE

ARMCHAIR FICTION
PO Box 4369, Medford, Oregon   97501-0168

*For more information about Armchair Books and products, visit our
website at…*

www.armchairfiction.com

Or email us at…

armchairfiction@yahoo.com

FINAL WEAPON

District Leader Howard Morely leaned back in his seat, to glance down at the bay. Idly, he allowed his gaze to wander over the expanse of water between the two blunt points of land, then he looked back at the skeletonlike spire which jutted upward from the green hills he had just passed over. He could remember when that ruin had been a support for one of the world's great bridges.

Now, a crumbling symbol of the past, it stubbornly resisted the attacks of the weather, as it had once resisted the far more powerful blasts of explosives. Obstinately, it pointed its rusty length skyward, to remind the observer of bygone conflict—and more.

Together with the tangled cables, dimly seen in the shoal water, the line of wreckage in the channel, and the weed-covered strip of torn concrete which led through the hills, it testified to the arrival of the air age. Bridges, highways, and harbors alike had passed their day of usefulness.

Not far from the ruined bridge support, Morely could see the huge, well maintained intake of one of the chemical extraction plants. He shook his head at the contrast.

"That eyesore should be pulled down," he muttered. "Should have been pulled down long ago. Suggested it in a report, but I suppose it never got to the Old Man. He depends on his staff too much. If I had the region, I'd—"

He shook his head. He was not the regional director—yet. Some day, the old director would retire. Then, Central Coördination would be examining the records of various district leaders, looking for a successor. Then—

He shrugged and turned his attention to his piloting of the borrowed helicopter. It was a clumsy machine, and he had to get in to Regional Headquarters in time for the morning conference. There would be no sense it getting involved in employee traffic—not if he could avoid it.

The conference, his informant had told him, would be a little out of the ordinary. It seemed that the Old Man had become somewhat irritated by the excess privileges allowed in a few of the eastern districts. And he was going to jack everyone up about it. After that would come the usual period of reports, and possibly a few special instructions. Some of the leaders would have pet projects to put forward, he knew. They always did. Morely smiled to himself. He'd have something to come up with, too.

And this conference might put a crimp in Harwood's style. Morely had carefully worded his progress report to make contrast with the type of report that he knew would come from District One. George Harwood had been allowing quite a few extra privileges to his people, stating that it was good for morale. And, during the past couple of months, he'd seemed to be proving his point. Certainly, the production of the employees from the peninsula had been climbing. Harwood, Morely decided would be the most logical person—after himself—for the region when the Old Man retired. In fact, for a time, it had looked as though the director of District One was going to be a dangerous rival.

But this conference would change things. Morely smiled slowly as he thought of possible ways of shading the odds.

He looked ahead. Commuters were streaming in from the peninsula now, to make for the factory parking lots. His face tightened a little. Why, he wondered, had the Old Man decided to call the conference at this hour? He could have delayed a little, until commuter traffic was less heavy. He'd been a district leader once. And before that, under the old government, a field leader. He should know how annoying the employee classes could be. And to force his leaders to mingle with commuting employees in heavy traffic!

FOR THAT matter, everyone seemed to be conspiring to make things uncomfortable today. Those heavy-handed mechanics in the district motor pool, for example. They'd failed him today. His own sleek machine, with its distinctive markings was still being repaired. And he'd been forced to use this unmarked security patrol heli. The machine wasn't really too bad, of course. It had a superb motor, and it carried identification lights and siren, which could be used if necessary. But it resembled some lower-class citizen's family carryall. And, despite its modifications, it still handled like one. Morely grimaced and eased the wheel left a little. The helicopter swung in a slow arc.

Helis were rising from the factory lots, to interlace with incoming ships before joining with the great stream headed south. The night workers were heading for home. Morely hovered his machine for a moment, to watch the ships jockey for position, sometimes barely avoiding collisions in the stream of traffic. He watched one ship, which edged forward, stopped barely in time to avoid being hit, edged forward again, and finally managed to block traffic for a time while its inept driver fooled with the controls and finally got on course.

"Quarrelsome, brawling fools," he muttered. "Even among themselves, they can't get along."

He looked around, noting that the air over the Administrative Group was comparatively free of traffic. To be sure, he would have to cross the traffic lines, but he could take the upper lanes, avoiding all but official traffic. A guard might challenge, but he could use his identifying lights. He wouldn't be halted. He corrected his course a little, glanced at the altimeter, and put his ship into a climb.

At length, he eased his ship over the parklike area over Administrative Square and hovered over the parking entry. A light blinked on his dash, to tell him that all the official spaces were occupied. He grunted.

"Wonder they couldn't leave a clear space in Official. They know I'm coming in for conference."

He moved the control wheel, allowing his ship to slide over to a shopping center parking slot, and hovered over the entry, debating. He could park here and take the sub-surface to Administrative, or he could use the surface lot just outside of the headquarters group. Of course, the director frowned on use of the surface lot, except in emergency. The underground lots were designated for all normal parking. Morely thought over the problem, ignoring the helis which hovered, waiting for him to clear the center of the landing area. Finally, his hand started for the throttle. He would settle in the landing slot, let the guards shove his heli to a space, and avoid any conflict with the director's orders regarding the surface lot.

SUDDENLY, THERE was a sputtering roar. Someone had become impatient at the delay. A small sports heli swept by, impellers reversed, and dropped rapidly toward the entry to the underground parking space. Morely's ship rocked a little in the air blast.

For an instant, Morely felt a sharp pain which gnawed at the pit of his stomach. His head was abruptly light, and his hand, apparently of its own volition, closed over the throttle knob.

This joy boy was overdue for a lesson.

Morely measured the distance quickly, judging the instant when the other pilot would have to repitch his impellers and halt his downward rush. He allowed his own heavy ship to wallow earthward.

Scant feet from ground surface, the sportster pilot flicked his pitch control and pulled his throttle out for the brief burst of power which would allow him to drop gently to the landing platform.

Morely grinned savagely as he saw the impellers below him change pitch and start to move faster. He twisted his own impellers to full pitch and pulled out the throttle for a sudden, roaring surge of power, then swung the control column, jerking his ship up and away. As he steadied his heli and cut power, he looked down.

The powerful downblast had completely upset the sportster pilot's calculations. The small ship, struck by the gale from above, had listed to the right and gone out of control, grazing one of the heavy splinter shutters at the side of the landing slot. The ship lay on its side, amidst the wreckage of its impellers.

Morely flicked on his warning siren and lights, then feathered his own impellers, dropping his ship in free fall. He dropped to the grassy area by the landing slot, ignoring the other ships which scattered like frightened chickens, to give him room. At the last instant, he twisted the impellers to full pitch again, pulled out the throttle for a moment, then slammed the lever to the closed position. His ship touched down on springy turf, its landing gear settling gently to accept the weight. A klaxon was sounding, and warning lights flashed from the landing slot, to warn ships away from an attempted landing.

It would be a long time before the shiny, new sportster would be in condition to sweep into another parking area. And, after paying his fine and taking care of his extra duties, it would be an even longer time before the employee-pilot would have much business in the luxury shopping center, anyway.

Morely smiled bitterly as he closed the door of his ship. It didn't pay to cross Howard Morely—ever.

He walked slowly toward the landing slot, motioning imperiously to an approaching guard.

"Have someone place that ship for me," he ordered, jerking a thumb back toward his heli. "Then come over to that wreck. I shall want words with the pilot." He held out his small identification folder.

The guard's glance went to the folder. For an instant, he studied the card exposed before him, then he straightened and saluted, his face expressionless.

"Yes, sir." He signaled another guard, then pointed toward Morely's ship, and to the landing slot. "I can go with you now."

The two went down in the elevator and walked over to the wrecked sportster. A slender man was crawling from a door. When the man was clear of his ship, Morely beckoned.

"Over here, Fellow," he commanded.

The sportster pilot approached, the indignation on his face changing to bewilderment, then dismay as he noted Morely's insignia and the attitude of the two men who faced him.

Morely turned to the guard.

"Get me his name, identification number, and the name of his leader."

"Yes, sir."

The guard turned to the man, who grimaced a little with pain as he slowly put a hand in his pocket. Wordlessly, he extracted a bulky folder, from which he took a small booklet. He held out the booklet to the guard.

Morely held out a hand. "Never mind," he said. "Simply put him in custody. I'll turn this over to his leader myself."

He had noted the cover design on the booklet. It was from District One—Harwood's district. He flipped the cover open, ascertaining that there was no transfer notice. He'd give this to Harwood all right—at the right time. He looked at his watch.

"I shall want my heli in about three hours," he announced. "See to it that it's ready. And have a man check the fuel and see if the ship's damaged in any way." He turned away.

THE DISTRICT leaders sat before the large conference table. Among them, close to the director's place, was Morely, his face fixed in an expression of alert interest. His informant had been right. The man must have gotten a look at the Old Man's notes. The regional director was criticizing the laxity in inspection and control of employee activities. He objected to the excessive luxury activity allowed to some members of the employee classes, as well as to the overabundance of leisure allowed in several cases, some of which he described in detail.

He especially pointed up the fact that a recent heli meet had been almost dominated by employee class entries. And he pointed out the fact that there was considerable rehabilitation work to be done in bombed areas. It could be done by employees, during their time away from their subsistence jobs. That was all community time, he reminded.

It was all very well, he said, to allow the second- and even third-class citizens a certain amount of leisure recreation. That kept morale up. But they were certainly not to be allowed any position of dominance, either individually, or as a class. That, he said, was something else again. It was precisely the sort of thing that had led to the collapse and downfall of many previous civilizations.

"Keep 'em busy," he ordered. "So busy they don't have time to think up mischief to get into. Remember, gentlemen, second- and third-class citizens have no rights—only privileges. And privileges may be withdrawn at any time."

He rapped sharply on the table and sat down, looking at the leader of District One.

One by one, the district leaders made their verbal reports of activity. Occasionally, questions of production or work quotas were brought up and decided. Morely waited.

At last, he made his own report, emphasizing the fact that his district had exceeded its quotas—subsistence, luxury, and rehabilitation—for the fourth consecutive quarter. He cited a couple of community construction projects he had ordered and which were well on the way to completion, and brought out the fact that his people, at least, were being inspected constantly and thoroughly.

Also, he suggested, if any time remained to be used, or if leisure activity threatened to become excessive, it might be well to turn some attention outside of the old urban areas. There was considerable bomb damage in the suburban and former farming areas, and the scrap from some of the ruined structures could be stockpiled for disposal to factories and community reclamation plants.

Further, a beautification program for the entire region might keep some of the employee class busy for some time. And some of the ex-farmers among the lower classes might find it pleasant to work once again with the soil, instead of their normal work in the synthetic food labs or machine shops. With the director's permission, he could start the program by removing the useless tower and wreckage at the bay channel, and by salvaging the metal from it. Of course, he admitted, it was a trifle beyond his own authority, since most of the channel was in District One. The regional director cast him a sharp glance, then considered the suggestion. At last, he nodded.

"It might be well," he decided. "Go ahead, Morely. Take care of that detail." He looked over at his executive. "Have Planning draw up something on salvage and beautification in the former rural areas," he ordered. He looked about the room.

"And the rest of you might try looking over your own districts. You don't have to wait for a directive, and every one of you can find some improvement that could be made. If it's a district line matter, submit some plan for mutual agreement to my office." He rose and went to the door.

Morely waited, watching George Harwood. The leader of District One gathered his papers, looked down the table for an instant, then went out. Morely followed him at a discreet distance.

As Harwood neared the door to the regional director's office, Morely caught up with him.

"Oh, Harwood," he said loudly. "Caught one of your people in a flagrant case of reckless flying this morning. Why don't you bear down a little on those fellows of yours? This one seemed to think he was winning a heli meet."

He held out the folder he had confiscated. "Here's his identification. I had the guards hold him for you. Second-class citizen. Must've had a lot of spare time, to get the luxury credits and purchase authorization for that ship of his."

Harwood looked at him, a faint expression of annoyance crossing his face. Then, he glanced at the open door nearby, and comprehension grew on his face. He took the folder, nodded wordlessly, and walked rapidly past Morely, who turned to watch him.

As Harwood swung through the door to an elevator, Morely smiled appreciatively. That had been a smart trick, he thought. Have to remember that one. No argument to disturb the Old Man. Not even positive proof that Morely hadn't been talking to empty space. But there was an answer to that, too, if one was alert. He walked through the doorway into the director's office.

The regional director looked up.

"Oh, Morely. You wanted to see me?"

"Yes, sir." Morely stood at rigid attention. "I just thought of all those useless highways around the countryside. Of course, a few of them have been camouflaged and converted to temporary and emergency heli parking lots, but there's still a lot of waste concrete about that could be removed. It would improve the camouflage of the groups. It could be divided into community projects for spare time work, sir."

"Very good idea. If this stalemate we're in should develop into another war, it would be well to have as few landmarks as possible. And some of these people do have too much time on their hands. They sit around, thinking of their so-called rights. Next thing we know, some of the second-class citizens'll be screaming for the privilege of a vote. Set it up in your district, Morely. We'll see how it works out, and the rest of the district leaders can follow your example."

He looked sharply at Morely. "Heard a little disturbance in the hall just before you came in."

"Oh, that." Morely contrived a look of confusion. "I'm sorry, sir. I didn't mean anyone to hear that. It was just that I had a minor bit of business with Leader Harwood. One of his people nearly knocked me out of the air this morning, over a parking area, and I confiscated his identification. I tried to give it to Harwood after the conference, but he must have been in a hurry. I caught up with him and gave him the folder."

"So I heard." The director smiled wryly. "Anything more?"

"No, sir." Morely saluted and left.

"That," he told himself, "should drop Harwood a few points."

He went to the parking area to reclaim his helicopter. Better get back to his district and start setting up those community projects. Too, he would have to run a check inspection or so this evening. See to it his sector men weren't getting lax. He'd check on Bond tonight.

HE FLEW back to District Twelve, dropped his helicopter into the landing area, and made his way to his office.

Inside, he went to a file, from which he took his spot-inspection folder. Carrying it to his desk, he checked it. Yes, Bond's sector was due for a spot inspection. Might be well to make a detailed check of one of the employees in that sector, too. Morely touched a button on his desk.

Almost immediately, a clerk stood in the doorway.

"Get me the master quarters file for Sector Fourteen," Morely ordered.

The clerk went out, to return with two long file drawers. Quickly, he set them side by side on a small table, which he pushed over to his superior's desk.

Idly, Morely fingered through the cards, noting the indexing and condition of the file. He nodded in approval, then gave the clerk a nod of dismissal. At least, his people were keeping their files in order.

He reached into a pocket, to withdraw a notebook. Turning its pages, he found a few of the entries he had made on population changes, then cross-checked them against the files. All were posted and properly cross-indexed. Again, he nodded in satisfaction.

Evidently, that last dressing down he had given the files section had done some good. For a moment, he considered calling in the chief clerk and complimenting him. Then, he changed his mind.

"No use giving him a swelled head," he told himself.

He drew a file drawer to him, running his finger down its length. At last, he pulled a card at random. It was colored light blue.

He put it back. Didn't want to check a group leader. He'd be a first-class citizen, and entitled to privacy. He pulled another card from a different section of the file. This one was salmon pink—an assistant group leader. He examined it. The man was a junior equipment designer in one of the communications plants. For a moment, Morely tapped the card against his desk. Actually, he had wanted a basic employee, but it might be well to check one of the leadmen. He could have the man accompany him while he made a further check on one of the apartments in his sub-group. Again, he looked at the card.

Paul Graham, he noted, was forty-two years of age. He had three children—was an electronics designer, junior grade. His professional profile showed considerable ability and training, but the security profile showed a couple of threes. Nothing really serious, but he would be naturally expected to be a second-class citizen—or below. It was not an unusual card.

Morely looked at the quarters code. Graham lived in Apartment 7A, Group 723, which was in Block 1022, Sector Fourteen. It would be well to check his quarters first, then check, say, 7E. Morely went through the numerical file, found the card under 7E, and flipped the pages of his notebook to a blank sheet, upon which he copied the data he needed from the two cards.

He put the notebook in his pocket and returned the cards to their places in the file, then riffled the entire file once more, to be sure there would be no clue as to which cards he had consulted. Finally, he touched the button on his desk again.

Once more, the clerk stood in the doorway.

"This file seems to be satisfactory," he was told. "You may bring in the correspondence now."

The correspondence was no heavier than usual. Morely flipped through the routine matter, occasionally selecting a report or letter and abstracting data. Tomorrow, he could check performance by referring to these. At last, he turned to the separate pile of directives, production and man-hour reports, and other papers which demanded more attention than the routine paper.

He worked through the stack of paper, occasionally calling upon his clerk for file data, sometimes making a communicator call. At last, he pushed away the last remaining report and leaned back. He spun his chair about, activated the large entertainment screen, and spent some time watching a playlet. At the end of the play, he glanced at his watch, then turned back to his desk. He leaned forward to touch a button on his communicator.

As the viewsphere lit, he flicked on the two-way video, then spoke.

"Get me Sector Leader Bond." He snapped the communicator off almost before the operator could acknowledge, then spun about, switching his entertainment screen to ground surface scan. A scene built up, showing a view from his estate in the hills.

THERE WERE some buildings on the surface—mostly homes of upper grade citizens, who preferred the open air, and could afford to have a surface estate in addition to their quarters in the groups. These homes, for the most part, were located in wooded areas, where their owners could find suitable fishing and hunting.

Most of the traces of damage done by the bombings of the Nineties were gone from about the estate areas by now, and the few which remained were being eliminated. Morely increased the magnification, to watch a few animals at a waterhole. He could do a little hunting in a few weeks. Take a nice leave. He drew a deep breath.

Those years after the end of the last war had been hectic, what with new organizational directives, the few sporadic revolts, the integration of homecoming fighters, and the final, tight set-up. But it had all been worth it. Everything was running smoothly now.

The second- and third-class citizens had learned to accept their status, and some few of them had even found they liked it. At least, now they had far more security. There was subsistence in plenty for all producers, thanks to the war-born advances in technology, and to the highly organized social framework. To be sure, a few still felt uneasy in the underground quarters, but the necessity for protection from bombing in another war had been made clear, and they'd just have to get used to conditions. And, there were a very few who, unable to get or hold employment, existed somehow in the Spartan discomfort of the subsistence quarters.

For most, however, there was minor luxury, and a plenitude of necessities. And there was considerable freedom of action and choice as well as full living comfort for the full citizens, who had proved themselves to be completely trustworthy, and who were deemed fit to hold key positions.

The communicator beeped softly, and he glanced at the sphere. It showed the face of Harold Bond, leader of the fourteenth sector. The district leader snapped on his scanner.

"Report to me here in my office at eighteen hours, Bond."

"Yes, sir."

"And you might be sure your people are all in quarters this evening."

Bond nodded. "They will be, sir."

"That's all." Morely flicked the disconnect switch.

He got up, strode around the office, then consulted his watch. There would be time for a cup of coffee before Bond arrived. Time for a cup of coffee, and time for the employees in Sector Fourteen to scurry about, getting their quarters in shape for an inspection. They would have no way of knowing which quarters were to be checked, and all would be put in order.

He smiled. It was a good way, he thought, to insure that there would be no sloppiness in the homes of his people. And it certainly saved a lot of inspection time and a lot of direct contact.

He went out of the office, and walked slowly down to the snack bar, where he took his time over coffee, looking critically at the neat counter and about the room as he drank.

The counter girls busied themselves cleaning up imaginary spots on the plastic counter and on their equipment, casting occasional, apprehensive glances at him. Finally, he set his cup down, looked at the clock over the counter, and walked out.

Bond was waiting in the office. Morely examined the younger man, carefully appraising his appearance. The sector leader, he saw, was properly attired. The neat uniform looked as if freshly taken from the tailor shop. The man stepped forward alertly, to halt at the correct distance before his superior.

"Good evening, sir. My heli is on the roof."

"Very good." Morely nodded shortly and took his notebook from his pocket. "We'll go to Building Seven Twenty-three."

He turned and walked toward the self-service elevator. Bond hurried a little to open the door for him.

BOND EASED the helicopter neatly through the entry slot and on down into one of the empty visitor spaces in the landing area at Block 1022. The two men walked across the areaway to an entrance.

As they went up the short flight of stairs into the hall, Morely took careful notice of the building. The mosaic tile of the stairs and floor gleamed from a recent scrubbing. The plastic and metal handrails were spotless. He looked briefly at his subordinate, then motioned toward the door at their right.

"This one," he ordered.

Bond touched the call button and they waited.

From inside the apartment, there was a slight rustle of motion, then the door opened and a man stood before them. For an instant, he looked startled, then he straightened.

"Paul Graham, sir," he announced. "Apartment 7A is ready for inspection." He stepped back.

Morely looked him over critically, saw nothing that warranted criticism, and went inside, followed by Bond.

Cursorily, the district leader let his gaze wander about the apartment. The kitchen at his left, he saw, was in perfect order, everything being in place and obviously clean. He went to the range and motioned with his head.

"Pull the drip pan," he ordered.

Graham came forward and pulled a flat sheet from the range, then opened an access door at the front of the stove.

Morely peered inside, then thrust a hand in. For a moment, he groped around, then he pulled his hand out and looked at it. It was clean. He sniffed at his fingers, then turned away.

"You may replace the pan, Fellow." He went into the living room, noting that the woman and three children were neat and in the proper attitudes of attention. One of the children was looking at him, wide-eyed. He saw that the child was clean and apparently healthy.

In addition to the usual chairs, table, and divan, there were some bookcases which formed a small alcove around a combination desk and drawing table. Morely circled the bookcases, to stand before the desk.

"What's this?" he demanded. He turned to a bookcase, to examine the titles.

Most of the books were engineering texts and reference works. There were some standard works of philosophy and a few on psychology. None of the titles seemed to be actually objectionable.

"I—" Graham started to speak, but Morely silenced him with an upraised hand.

"Later," he said coldly. "Bond, has this been reported to you, and have you investigated?"

Bond nodded. "Yes, sir," he said. "Graham is a design engineer, sir, and has been granted permission to do some research in his quarters.

"He's commercially employed, sir, and it was a routine matter. His employer says he has been keeping his production quotas, no alteration to the apartment has been made, and no community property has been defaced. I'm told that several of Graham's designs have been of value in his plant. I didn't think—"

"I see you didn't. What is this man working on now?"

"A new type of communicator, sir. I don't know all the details."

"Get them, Bond. Get them all, and give me a full report on his project and its progress tomorrow. Since this work is being done during time when the man is not working for his employer, he's using community time and the community becomes vitally interested in his results." Morely paused, looking at the bookcase again.

"And, while we are on the subject," he added, "get me details on those previous designs you spoke of. It's quite possible the community has not been getting royalty payments to which it's entitled." He picked out a book, flipping over its pages for a moment, then replaced it and looked searchingly at Bond.

"And get me a full inventory of this man's books and any equipment he may have." He turned on Graham.

"Do you have purchase authorization and receipts for all of this?"

"Yes, sir." Graham motioned toward the desk.

"Very well. I shan't bother with that now. An investigating team can check that."

Morely took a final glance at the half-finished schematic on the drawing board, then circled the bookcases again, to come out into the main room.

"We'll inspect the rest of your quarters."

AT LAST, Morely left the quarters area, followed by Bond. As they reached the helicopter, Morely turned, one hand on the door.

"Laxity, Bond, is something I don't tolerate. You should know that. Possibly this man, Graham, is doing nothing illegal, or even irregular. Possibly, he is not wasting community time, but I have very serious doubts. I'll venture to say the community has a financial interest in several of his recent designs, and I mean to find out which ones and how much. And it's certainly an unusual situation. The man's a leadman, you know, and could spend his time more profitably in checking on the people he's responsible for." He slid into the seat.

"I'll concede," he continued, "that employees are to be allowed a certain amount of recreation of their own choosing. They may have light reading in their quarters, and they may even work on small projects—with permission, of course. But this man seems to have gone much farther than that. He has a small electronics factory of his own, as well as a rather extensive library. He's obviously spending a lot of time at his activities, and that time must come out of his community performance. This certainly is not routine, and I can't condone your failure to make a report on it."

"But, I—"

Morely held up a hand sternly. "Let's not have a string of excuses," he said. "Give me a full report on the man's possessions, his history, and the progress of whatever work he's doing in that private factory of his. Get the details on his previous designs, too. And bring your report in to me in the morning, personally. I shall want to determine whether to make this new device a community project, or whether to allow it to be offered to his employer on a community royalty agreement. And I shall require details on his older designs for Fiscal to examine into. Research, you should know, is a community function, not something to be done in any set of quarters. I shall want to talk to you further when I've gone over this matter.

"Now, get me back to the district offices. I want to get home, and you've work to do tonight."

THE REPORT was a long one. Morely smiled to himself as he thought of the time it must have taken Bond to assemble the data and to make up his final draft. Possibly in the future, that young man would be a little less inclined to assume too much authority, or to be too soft in his dealings with the employee classes. The spring in his swivel chair twanged musically as the district leader leaned back to read.

First, there was an inventory of Graham's effects. It was a lengthy list, followed by a certification by a security inspector that all of the equipment inventoried was covered by authorizations and receipts held by Graham, and that none of the books and equipment were of improper nature for possession by a member of the employee classes. Morely grunted and tossed that section aside.

There was a detailed history of Graham's activities, so far as known to Security. Morely scanned through it hurriedly. There was nothing here of an unusual nature.

Graham had been graduated from one of the large technical colleges during the early nineties. Morely noted that it was one of those schools which had been later closed as a result of one of the post-war investigations.

The subject had been employed by Consolidated Electronics as a junior engineer, and had designed several improvements for Consolidated's products. There was a record of promotions and a few awards. He had held a few patents, which had been taken over by the Central Coördination Products Division during the post-war reorganization. He had also belonged to the now proscribed Society of Electronic Engineers, had contributed articles to that organization's journal, and had taken an active part in some of its chapter meetings.

During the war, he had worked on radio-controlled servos, doing acceptable work. When the professional and trade societies and other organizations were outlawed, he had promptly resigned from his society, and made the required declarations. But he had been reported as privately remarking that it was "a sad thing to see the last vestiges of personal freedom removed."

Morely pursed his lips. Not an unusual history, he decided. Of course, the man was completely ineligible for full citizenship—bad risk. He was barely qualified for second-class citizenship, his obvious ability being the only qualifying factor. Unlike many, he had no record of any effort to shirk duty, or do economic damage during the critical period. The district leader tossed the dossier aside and picked up the report on Graham's present activities.

There were a series of complex schematics, and several machine drawings which he shuffled to the back of his report. Those could be interpreted later, if necessary. He was interested in the description of function.

The device Graham was working on was described as a communicator which operated by direct mind-to-mind transfer. Morely sat up straighter, reading the paragraph over again. Either this man was a true genius, who had discovered a new principle, or he was completely a crackpot.

"Telepathy!"

Morely snorted and went over to the descriptions of the device, reading carefully. Finally, he read the comments of a senior engineer, who cautiously admitted that the circuits involved, though highly unconventional, were not of a type to cause spurious radiation, or to interfere with normal communication in any way.

The engineer also noted that it was possible that the device might be capable of radiation effects outside of the electromagnetic spectrum, and that the power device was capable of integration into standard equipment—in fact, might be well worth adoption. He carefully declined, however, to give any definite opinion without an actual model to run tests on. And he added the comment that the first model was as yet incomplete.

Morely tossed the last sheet to his desk and leaned forward, tapping idly on the dull-finished plastic. Finally, he touched his call button and waited till the clerk came in.

"You may send Mr. Bond in now," he directed.

He picked up the section of the report dealing with Graham's past designs, and started scanning it. He would have the Fiscal chief go over this and set up the necessary royalty agreements with Consolidated. Some of them might generate worth-while amounts of funds.

HE MADE no sign of recognition or awareness when Bond entered the office, but continued with his reading. At last, he pulled a notepad to him, wrote a brief endorsement to the Fiscal chief, and clipped it to the part of the report dealing with Graham's older designs. He replaced his pen in its stand and leaned back, to stare at his junior, who stood at rigid attention.

"Yes?"

"Sector Leader Bond, sir, reporting as ordered." Bond saluted.

Negligently, Morely returned the salute, then picked up Bond's report.

"I have gone through this, Bond," he announced. "Very interesting. And you thought it too unimportant to report on before?"

"I didn't want to bother you with some idle fantasy, sir. Until the man's experiments showed definite results of some sort, I—"

"And then, you hoped to spring a completed device on me? Take credit for it yourself, eh?"

"Not at all, sir. I—"

Morely raised a hand. "Never mind. I don't need any kind of aid to read your intentions. They're quite plain, I see. It would have been quite a credit to you, wouldn't it?

"'Look what I worked out, with a little, minor help from one of the employees in my sector.'

"But I've seen that line worked before, Bond, and worked smoothly. You don't catch the Old Man napping so easily as that." He paused.

"Of course we don't know whether or not this device is going to be of any real use. But we do know that this man,

Graham, has developed one thing which can be profitably incorporated into conventional equipment. That power source of his appears to be quite practical, and we'll adopt it. Offer it to the man's employer, subject to community royalty. And see if you can get Graham a little time off work in compensation. Then, keep a close watch on his work on the rest of his device. He'll probably use his time off to work on it—at least, he'll be a lot better off if he does.

"I want frequent reports on his progress—daily reports, if any significant developments occur. And I want a model of that device as soon as it's developed and has had preliminary tests. If it works, it might be valuable for community defense." He waved a hand.

"That's all."

Bond turned to go, and almost got to the door before Morely called him back.

"Oh, one more thing, Bond. Keep a closer watch on the rest of your people. If any more of them decide to do extra work of any unusual nature, I shall expect an immediate report in full. Don't fail me again. Is that clear?"

"Yes, sir." Bond saluted again and made his escape.

Morely watched him disappear, then turned to his communicator. "Get me Field Leader Denton," he ordered.

The pause was slight, then the face of a middle-aged man appeared in the viewsphere.

"Denton," said the district leader, "I want you to keep closer watch on your sector men. Last night I spot-checked Bond, in Fourteen, and I found an irregularity. I'll expect you to endorse the report back, and I'll expect you to tighten down. Keep an especially close eye on this man, Bond."

The field leader's eyebrows raised a little. "Bond, sir? He's one of—"

"Bond. Yes." His superior interrupted forcefully. "And tighten down on all your men. You know how I feel about laxity."

He snapped the communicator off and gathered Bond's report together. For a few seconds, he looked at the neat stack of paper, then he slipped a paper clamp on it and punched his call button.

"THERE!" PAUL Graham straightened from his hunched-over position at the desk. He laid his soldering iron down and massaged the small of his back, grimacing slightly.

"Oh, me! I'll swear my back'll never be the same again. But that ought to do it, at last." He looked at the equipment before him and grinned ruefully.

"Of all the haywire messes. It started out so nice. And it ended up so awful."

The device *had* started out as a fairly neat assembly, using a headband as a chassis. But the circuitry seemed to have gone out of control. Miniature sub-assemblies hung at all angles from their wires and tiny components were interlaced through the unit, till the entire assembly looked like a wig from a horror play. Graham shook his head, picked up the band; and carefully fitted it, being careful that the contacts touched his forehead and temples properly.

For an instant, he looked a little dazed. Then, he reached up and fumbled for a moment with the controls at the front of the headband. Suddenly, he stopped, an expression of pleasure on his face. He stood for a time, looking at the wall, then looked up at the ceiling. He frowned and looked at his wife, who was anxiously watching him. A smile grew on his face, and she was clearly conscious of the projected thought.

"*I told you, Elaine, it can't possibly hurt anyone. Stop worrying about me.*"

Elaine Graham looked startled. "I didn't, say anything, darling."

Her husband looked at her with an impish grin. She frowned a little, then her eyes widened and her mouth opened a little. She ran at him indignantly.

"It simply isn't decent! You take that thing off, Paul Graham, right now. I won't have you reading my mind!"

Graham laughingly fended her off with one hand as he carefully removed the headband with the other. He set the device gently on the desk, then seized his wife about the waist.

"It works, honey," he said jubilantly. "It really works." He waltzed her away from the desk, to the middle of the living room.

"Of course, I couldn't get anything from anyone but you. It seems to work just as I thought it might—only if you can see the person you want to contact. But I'll bet two people who were acquainted could use two of these things to communicate with each other at any distance. And it may be possible to work out the problem of single-device communication at distance and through obstacles. But that'll have to come later. Right now, this thing works."

"But Paul. I'm afraid. What will *they* do with something like this? We have so little freedom left now. Why, they won't even let us think privately." She paused, her head turning from side to side as she looked about the apartment.

"You know, Paul, I hardly ever dare go out of this apartment now, they upset me so. And if they're able to read my thoughts, I shan't be safe, even here."

Graham frowned. "True," he admitted. "But somehow, when I had the thing on, I got some funny ideas. I wonder if anyone could really oppress someone he fully understood. I wonder if two people who could fully comprehend each other's point of view could have a really serious disagreement." He picked up the headband, looking at it searchingly.

"AND THERE'S another thing," he added. "Unless both parties are wearing the things, vision seems to be essential to any reaction, at least in this model. I tried to get thoughts from the kids and from the Moreno's, upstairs. But there wasn't a thing. And yet, I could get you clearly. Apparently this thing won't work out as a spy device."

"But, are you sure?"

Graham shrugged wryly. "Well...no," he admitted. "I'll have to finish wiring the other set and try 'em both out before I'll be sure of anything. And it'll take a lot of tests before I'm sure of very much. Now, I've just got some ideas." He frowned thoughtfully.

"Anyway, I can't stop now. They know about the thing, and I've got to finish it—or furnish definite proof it's impractical." He turned back to the desk. "Should be through with the other band in a few minutes. Just have to put in a couple of filters."

He picked up the completed device and turned around again. "Here, Elaine, put this on, will you? See what you get. Try to catch a thought from outside the room."

DUTIFULLY, ELAINE Graham accepted the headband. She eyed it doubtfully for a moment, then adjusted it over her hair, setting the contacts on her skin as she had seen her husband do. For a few seconds, she stared at her husband, wide-eyed. Then, she looked away, her eyes focused on infinity.

Graham busied himself with the soldering iron and another headband.

At last, Elaine took the headband off. "It's weird, Paul," she said. "When I was looking at you, I knew everything you were thinking. But when I looked away, there was nothing. It was almost as though I didn't have it on. Only, I seemed to be able to think so much more clearly."

Graham looked up from his work, squinting thoughtfully. "Yeah," he muttered. "Yeah, I noticed that, too, come to think of it. Feedback effect of some sort, I suppose. Have to experiment with that, too, I expect." He turned back to his work.

ELAINE PUT the headband back on and watched him. She felt a complete familiarity with everything he was working on. For the first time, she felt she fully understood this man with whom she had lived for so many years. And the understanding was pleasant. She could comprehend the mysteries of the circuits he was working on. She had always felt slightly neglected when he worked with his equipment, especially since the bureaucracy, who took his results without recompense. Now, she could feel his interest in his work for its own sake. She could sympathize with it. And, with a little study, she felt she could join with him.

Graham straightened again. "It's done," he said. He picked the second headband from the desk and put it on. Abruptly, both he and his wife were aware of a fuzziness in their thoughts and senses. The walls, the floor, and the furniture seemed to blur and waver, like the fantasy world of delirium. He put his hand up and adjusted the controls. The room returned to normal, and their senses were abruptly sharp and clear again. He dropped his hand.

"Outside. See if it'll work when we can't see each other."

"Almost curfew time."

"Only a couple of minutes. Then lights out and sleep."

Elaine walked to the door. She stepped out into the corridor and walked down the steps.

"All right?"

"Perfect! Try the parking lot. Close the door."

She went out of the quarters, crossed the areaway, and stood under the landing slot. Far overhead, a segment of sky appeared between the open bomb shutters. Stars shone coldly. She was conscious of a movement and looked down, toward a shadow which moved among the parked helicopters.

"What's that?"

She looked more closely at the shadow, then shuddered a little.

"Never mind." The thought was urgent. *"Come inside. I got him, too."*

QUICKLY, ELAINE walked back into the apartment. She closed the door and walked to the desk, removing the headband as she approached. Her husband put his headband beside it.

"We'd better get to bed," he said quietly. "I'll notify them tomorrow."

"No, Paul. It would be harder then. And there would be so many questions. Call the sector leader tonight. We'll have to get it over." Elaine shivered.

"But what *will* they do with it?" She asked the question almost despairingly.

Graham shook his head. "I'm not sure," he admitted. "I started with the idea of simply building a really effective communicator. But this is more than that. To you and I, it meant full understanding. But to that person out there...I don't know."

"His thoughts were flat—almost lifeless. And he made my skin crawl. Paul, do you remember how you used to feel when you came close to a snake? There's something wrong with that man."

"I know. I felt it, too. And it made the blood rush into my ears." Graham moved toward the communicator, placing his hand on the switch. "And you're right. I'll have to report immediately. They don't really need telepathy. And certainly, they never required real evidence. A suspicion is sufficient, and they'd be very suspicious if I didn't notify the sector leader tonight."

He depressed the switch deliberately, like a man firing a weapon. Then, he dialed a number, and waited.

The sphere lit, to show the face of Harold Bond.

"Oh, Graham." Bond frowned a little. "It's late. Do you have something to report?"

"Yes, sir." Graham's face was expressionless. "The mental communicator is finished. Do you wish to test it, sir?"

Bond opened his eyes a little more and nodded. "It's really done, then?"

"Yes, sir."

"I'll be there in a few minutes." The sphere darkened.

Graham looked at it. De-energized, the communicator seemed to be merely a large ball of clear material. It stood on its low pedestal, against its black background, reflecting a distorted picture of the chiaroscuro of the room. He leaned toward it, and saw a faint, deformed reflection of his own head and shoulders.

He spread his hands a little, and turned around. Elaine had crossed to the divan, where she sat, looking apathetically at the door, her hands folded in her lap. He smiled apprehensively, coughed, and held up a hand, two fingers crossed.

Elaine glanced at him, nodded, and resumed her watch of the door. Graham shrugged and walked over to his desk, where he stood, aimlessly looking down at the two headbands.

THEY BOTH jumped convulsively when the buzzer sounded. Graham strode rapidly to the door, opened it, and stood back as the sector leader came in. Elaine had come to her feet, and stood rigidly, facing the door.

Sector Leader Bond closed the door, then looked from one of them to the other. He shook his head a little sadly, and waved a hand gently back and forth.

"Relax, you two," he said. "I'm alone this time." He turned to Graham. "Let's see what we've got."

Graham walked to his desk and picked up the two headbands.

"They're a little rough-looking, sir," he apologized. "But they work."

Bond tossed his head back with a little laugh. "They do look a little rugged, don't they?" he chuckled. "Well, we'll worry about appearance later. Right now, I'm curious. I want to see what these things do."

Graham handed over one of the bands and slowly adjusted the other to his head. For a moment, he looked searchingly at the sector leader, then his face relaxed into a relieved expression.

"*Hear me?*"

Bond had been examining the device in his hands. He looked up, puzzled.

"Of course I hear you," he said. "I'm not deaf."

Graham smiled a little, then placed a hand tightly over his mouth.

"*Still get me?*"

Bond cocked his head to one side, looked down at the device in his hands, then looked up again. "Well," he commented. "So that's the way they work. I thought you spoke."

Graham shook his head. "*Didn't have to. Try it on.*"

Bond shrugged. "Well, here we go." He pulled off his cap, tossed it to a chair, and replaced it with the headband. For a moment, he looked around the apartment, then he glanced at Mrs. Graham. He blinked, ducked his head, and looked more closely at her.

"*Ow! Nobody could be as bad as that!*" He looked at Graham. "*What do you think?*"

"*There's one outside.*" Graham inclined his head a little.

Elaine Graham sprang to her feet. "I'm terribly sorry," she apologized contritely. "It's just that I—"

Bond took off the headband abruptly. "I'm sorry, too," he said. "I was prying." He looked down at the device. "I'm not too sure about this thing," he added. "It works. I can see that much. But I'm almost afraid it works too well. What's it going to cause?"

Graham pulled off his own headband and extended his hand for the other. "I'm not sure," he admitted. "I'm not sure of anything at all." He frowned. "Wish I hadn't—" He looked at the sector leader quickly.

"I'm sorry, sir," he apologized. "Forgot my training, I guess."

Bond waved a hand. "Look," he said, "there are times, and there are places. Right now, I'm in your home, and I'm just as worried about this as you are. I'm just another person." He looked down at his neat uniform.

"Once," he mused, "we were all just people. Now—" He shrugged. "And then, these things come along." He looked at the two headbands, then at the man holding them.

"Wonder how many people feel like that?"

Graham held out the headbands. "I know one way to find out."

Bond nodded. "I see what you mean," he admitted. "But it could be pretty bad." He walked over to the chair and picked up his cap.

"Well," he added with a sigh, "I suppose I'd better grab these things and take them over to Research. Have to find out all we can about them. I've still got to report on them." Again, he looked at Graham. "You'd better come along, too. Research people might have a lot of questions, and I could never answer them."

GRAHAM NODDED and went to the hall closet. He took his coat from the hanger, put it on, and reached for his hat, then hesitated.

"You know," he said, "we might try one experiment, right here."

"Oh?" Bond raised his eyebrows.

"There's a man out in the parking lot. I believe he's detailed to keep watch on me. You might try him with one of the headbands. Then, see what he'll do with one on."

"Any special reason?"

Graham twisted his face uneasily. "I can't describe it," he said almost inaudibly. "You'd have to see for yourself."

Bond looked at him speculatively for a moment, then held out his cap and one of the headbands.

"Here, hold these."

He put the other headband on, accepted the first, and walked out of the apartment, followed by Graham, who still carried the cap.

As they came out and started across the parking lot, a man approached them.

Bond looked at him, frowned, then cast a sidelong look at Graham.

"*That what you meant?*" His thought carried an undercurrent of incredulity.

Graham nodded wordlessly, and Bond looked toward the approaching man again. Once more, his face wrinkled distastefully, then he spoke aloud.

"Oh, Ross. Want you to try some thing." He held out the headband he was carrying in his left hand.

Ross came up, accepted the device, and looked at it curiously. "You mean this is the thing he's been working on?" He jerked a thumb at Graham. "Saw his wife come out a while ago. Guess she had one of 'em on. She went right back in again."

Bond nodded. "This is it," he said. "Let's see how it works for you."

Ross shrugged. "Try anything once, I guess." He adjusted the band to his head, then stood, looking at the two men.

"*Notice anything?*" Bond looked at him sharply.

Again, Ross shrugged. "Nothing special," he said with a slight grunt. "Seems as though this guy's pretty nervous."

"*You don't have to say anything, just think it. And see if you can communicate with Graham.*"

"Huh?" Ross had been looking directly at Bond. He frowned.

"*You mean, this thing—*" He paused, looking for a moment at Graham, then took the headband off. "Thing doesn't feel good," he complained. He held the device out to Bond, who accepted it.

"But it works? You could communicate both ways with it?"

"Oh, sure." Ross nodded grudgingly. "I got you, all right. But I couldn't get a thing out of this guy." He wagged his head toward Graham. "Except he was jittery about something."

"I see. Thanks." Bond accepted the headband. "We're going to take these to Research," he added. "Let the technicians there find out how good they are." He turned away and led Graham to his helicopter.

As Graham settled in the seat, he turned to the sector leader. "He just couldn't use it properly," he remarked. "Maybe only certain people *can* use them."

Bond nodded as he started the motor. "Or maybe only certain people can't." He busied himself in getting the machine up through the landing slot, then turned as they climbed into the night sky.

"Maybe you've got to be able to understand and like people before you can establish full contact with them. Maybe... Maybe a lot of things." He was silent for a moment. "You know, this thing might become far more valuable than you thought, Graham."

HOWARD MORELY looked up from a memo as the clerk tapped on the door.

"Come in."

The man opened the door and stepped inside.

"Sector Leader Bond is here, sir. He has some gentlemen with him."

"And what does he want?"

"He said it was about that new communicator, sir."

"Oh." Morely turned his attention back to the memo. "Have them wait." He waved a hand in dismissal and went on with his reading.

The beautification program was progressing well. Twenty miles of the old main highway through the valley had been completely cleared and planted. Crews were working on another stretch. The foreman of the wrecking crew down at the point, in Sector Nine, reported that the last bit of scrap had been removed from the old bridge support. Underwater crews had salvaged the cables and almost all of the metal from the fallen bridge itself, and the scrap was on the beach, ready for delivery to the reclamation mills in District One.

Morely smiled sourly. Harwood would have a storage problem on his hands in a day or so. The delay in delivery could be explained and justified. Morely had seen to that. Now, all the material was ready and could be delivered in one lot.

Harwood would have to raise his production quota in his community mills to use up the excess material, and that would slow down the clean-up in District One. The Old Man couldn't help but notice, and he'd see who was efficient in his region. The district leader pushed the memo sheets aside and placed his hands behind his head.

Slowly, he pivoted his chair, to look at the entertainment screen. He started to energize it, then drew his hand back.

So that crackpot, Graham, had finally come up with something definite. Morely smiled again. It had almost seemed as though the man had been stalling for a while. But the pressure and the veiled threats had been productive— again.

To be sure, the agents covering that project had reported that the device seemed to be merely another fairly good means of communication—nothing of any tremendous importance. But results had been obtained, and a communicator which was reasonably free from interception and which required relatively low power might be of some value to the community. He might be able to get a commendation out of it, at least.

And even if it were unsuitable for defense, there'd be a new product for one of the luxury products plants in the district, and the district would get royalties from the manufacturer. Too, it would keep people busy and make 'em spend more of their credits.

He grimaced at his vague reflection in the screen before him, and spoke aloud.

"That's the way to get things done. Make 'em know who's in charge. And let 'em know that no nonsense will be tolerated. Breathe down their necks a little. They'll produce." He cleared his throat and spun around, to punch the button on his desk.

THE DOOR opened and the clerk stood, respectfully awaiting orders.

"Send in Bond and the people with him."

The clerk stepped back, turning his head.

"You may go in now, sir." He disappeared around the door.

Harold Bond stepped through the doorway, followed by two men. Morely looked at them closely. Engineers, he thought.

"What have you got?" he demanded.

One of the men opened a briefcase and removed a large, dully gleaming band. Apparently, it was made of plastic, or some light alloy, for he handled it as though it weighed very little.

As the man laid it on the desk, Morely examined the object closely. It was large enough to go on a man's head, he saw. It had adjustable straps, which could be used to hold it in place, and there were a few spring-loaded contacts, which apparently were meant to rest against a wearer's forehead and temples.

A few tiny knobs protruded from one side of the band, and a short wire, terminated by a miniature plug, depended from the other.

The engineer dipped into his brief case again, to produce a small, flat case with a long wire leading from it. He put this by the headband, and connected the plugs.

"The band, sir," he explained, "is to be worn on the head." He pointed to the flat case. "To save weight in the band, we built a separate power unit. It can be carried in a pocket. We've tested the unit, sir, and it does provide a means of private communication with anyone within sight, or with a group of people. Two people, wearing the headbands, can communicate for considerable distances, regardless of obstacles."

"I see." Morely picked up the headband. "Do you have more than one of these?"

"Yes, sir. We made four of the prototypes and tested them thoroughly." Bond stepped forward. "I sent a report in on them yesterday."

"Yes, yes. I know." Morely waved impatiently. He examined the headband again. "And you say it provides communication?"

"Yes, sir."

"No chance of interception?"

Bond shook his head. "Well," he admitted, "if two people are in contact, and a third equipped person wishes to contact either one, he can join the conversation."

"So, it's easier to tap than a cable circuit, or even a security type radio circuit." Morely frowned. "Far from a secure means of communication."

"Well, sir, if anyone cuts in on a communication, both parties know it immediately."

Morely grunted and shook his head. "Still not secure," he growled. He looked at the papers on his desk. "Oh, put one on. We'll see how they work." He leaned back in his chair.

BOND TURNED to the man with the brief case, who held out another headband. The sector leader fitted it to his head, plugged in the power supply and looked around the room. Finally, he glanced at his superior. A shadow of uncertainty crossed his face, followed by a quickly suppressed expression of distaste.

Morely watched him. "Well?" he demanded impatiently, "I don't feel or see anything unusual."

"Of course not, sir," explained Bond smoothly. "You haven't put on the other headband yet."

"Oh? I thought you could establish communication with only one headset, so long as you were in the same room."

Bond smiled ingratiatingly. "Only sometimes, sir. Some people are more susceptible than others."

"I see." Morely looked again at the headband, then set it on his head. One of the engineers hurried forward to help him with the power pack, and he looked around the room, becoming conscious of slight sensations of outside thought. As he glanced at the engineers, he received faint impressions of anxious interest.

"Can you receive me, sir?"

Morely looked at Bond. The younger man was staring at him with an intense expression on his face. The district leader started to speak, then remembered and simply thought the words.

"Of course I can. Didn't you expect results?"

"Oh, certainly, sir. Do you want me to go outside for a further test?"

The headband was bothering Morely a little. Unwanted impressions seemed to be hovering about, uncomfortably outside the range of recognition. He took the device off and looked at it again.

"No," he said aloud. "It won't be necessary. It's obvious to me that this thing will never be any good for practical application in any community communications problem. It's too vague. But it'll make an interesting toy, I suppose. Some people might like it as a novelty, and it'll give them some incentive to do extra work in order to own one. That's what luxury items are for. And the district can use any royalty funds it may generate."

He laid the headband on his desk. "Go ahead and produce a few samples. Offer the designs to Graham's employer. He can offer them on the luxury market, if he wishes, and we'll see what they do. If people want them, it might be profitable, both for the district and for Consolidated." He shrugged.

"No telling what'll make people spend their credits." He started to nod a dismissal, then hesitated.

"Oh, yes. I think I'll keep this one," he added. "And you might leave a couple more. The regional director might be amused by them."

He accepted the two headbands and their power packs, put them in a desk drawer, and sat back to watch the three men leave the office.

AFTER THE door closed, he still sat, idly staring at the headband on his desk. He put it on his head again, then sat, looking about the room. There was no unusual effect, and he took the band off again, looked at it sourly, and laid it down.

Somehow, when Bond and those other two had been in the room, he had sensed a vague feeling of expectancy. Those three had seemed to be enthusiastic and hopeful about something, he was sure. But he failed to see what. This headband certainly showed him nothing.

He stared at the band for a while longer, then put it back on and punched the call button on his desk. As his clerk came into sight, he watched the man closely. There *was* a slight effect. He could sense a vague fear. And a little, gnawing hatred. But nothing was definite, and no details of thought came through. He shrugged.

Of course the man was fearful. He probably was reviewing his recent mistakes, wondering which one he might be called upon to explain. Too bad his mind wasn't clear enough to read. But what could you expect? Possibly, he could drive Research into improving the device later.

"Anyway," he told himself, "everyone has something they're afraid of. It's natural. And everyone has their pet hates, too." For an instant, he thought of Harwood.

He focused his mind on a single thought. *"Get me the quarters file for Sector Nine."*

There was a definite effect this time. There was a sharp radiation of pained surprise. Then, there was acquiescence. The clerk started to say something, then backed toward the door. The impression of fear intensified. Morely smiled sardonically. The thing was an amusing toy, at that. He might find uses for it.

He sat back, thinking. He could use it as a detector. Coupled with shrewd reasoning, well-directed questions, and his own accurate knowledge of human failings, it could tell him a great deal about his people and their activities.

For instance, a question about some suspicious circumstance would cause a twinge of fear from the erring person. And that could be detected and localized. Further questions would produce alternate feelings of relief and intensified fear. He nodded complacently. Very little had ever gotten by him, he thought. But from now on, no error would remain undiscovered or unpunished.

The clerk returned to place the file drawers convenient to his superior's desk. He hesitated a moment, his eyes on the headband, then picked up the completed papers from the desk and went out.

Morely riffled through the cards, idly checked a few against his notes, and leaned back again. The file section seemed to be operating smoothly. He looked at his desk. Everything that had to be done immediately was done. And the morning was hardly more than half over.

He rose to his feet. Surely, somewhere in the headquarters, there must be some sort of trouble spot. Somewhere, someone was not producing to the fullest possible. There must be some loose end. And he'd find it. He went out, jerking a thumb back at his office as he passed his clerk's desk.

"You can pick up those files again, Roberts. And see to it that my office gets cleaned up a little. I won't be back for a while."

He went out, to walk down the corridor to the snack bar.

THERE WERE a few girls there. He walked by their table, glancing at their badges. Communications people. He nodded to himself, ordered coffee, and chose a table.

As he glanced at the girls' table, he could detect a current of uneasiness. They'd probably been fooling away more time than they should. Too bad he couldn't get more definite information from their thoughts. Like to know just how long they had been there. He tilted his wrist, taking a long look at his watch. The current of uneasiness increased. No doubt to it, they'd been more than ten minutes already.

The girls hurriedly finished their coffee and left. Morely sipped at his own cup.

At last, he got up and went out. Might be a good idea to visit the Fixed Communications Section. Looked as though there might be a little laxity there.

As he walked down the corridor, he mentally reviewed the operation of communications. There was Fixed Communications, responsible for communicator service to all the offices and quarters in the district, as well as to the various commercial organizations. There were also Mobile Comm, Warning, Long Lines, and Administrative Radio.

Of these, the largest was Fixed Communications, with its dial equipment, its banks of video amplifiers, the network of cables, and the substation equipment. It would take days to thoroughly check all their activities. But the office was the key to the entire operation. He could check their records, and get a clue to their efficiency. And he could question the section chief.

He took the elevator to the communications level and walked slowly along the hallway, glancing at the heavy steel door leading to Warning as he passed it. That could be checked later, though there would be little point to it.

It had always annoyed him to think of the operators in that section. They simply sat around, doing nothing but watch their screens and keep their few, piddling records. They did nothing productive, but they had to be retained. Actually, he had to admit, they were a necessity under present conditions. War was always a possibility and the enemy was building up his potential. He might strike at any time, and he'd certainly not send advance notification. If he did strike, the warning teams would perform their brief mission, alerting the active, working members of the defense groups. Then, they would be available for defense. And the defense coördinators required warning teams and equipment in prescribed districts. His was one of these.

He grumbled to himself. Even the number of operators and their organization were prescribed. This was a section, right within his own district, where he had little authority. And it was irritating. Drones, that's what they were.

He continued to the Fixed Communications office. Here, at least, he had authority.

He walked through the door, casting a quick glance at the office as he entered. The section chief got up from his chair, and came forward. Morely felt a little glow of satisfaction as he detected the now familiar aura of uneasiness. Again, he wished this device he wore were more effective. He would like to know the details of this man's thoughts.

"GOOD MORNING, sir." The Fixed Communication chief saluted.

Morely returned the salute perfunctorily, then examined the man critically.

"Morning," he acknowledged. "Kirk, I want you to get some new uniforms. You look like a rag bag."

A little anger was added to the uneasiness. Kirk looked down at his clothing. It wasn't new, but there was actually little wrong, other than the slight smudge on a trouser leg, and a few, small spots of dullness on his highly polished boots.

"I've been inspecting some cable vaults, sir," he explained. "We had a little trouble, due to ground seepage."

"It makes no difference," the district leader snorted, "what you've been doing. A man in your position should be properly attired at all times." He paused, looking Kirk over minutely. "If your cable vaults are in such bad condition, get them cleaned up. When I look your installations over, I shall expect them to be clean. Clean, and in order."

He looked beyond Kirk. "And get that desk cleared. A competent man works on one thing at a time and keeps his work in order. A place for everything, and everything in its place, you know. You don't need all that clutter. Is the rest of your office as disorderly as this?"

He looked disparagingly about the small room, then turned toward the door to the main communications office. Kirk moved to open the door.

At one side of the large office was a battery of file cabinets. Four desks were arranged conveniently to them. Morely looked at this arrangement.

"What's this?"

"Billing and Directory, sir. These are the master files of all fixed communication subscribers. From them, we make up the semiannual directory, its corrective supplements, and the monthly bills."

Morely frowned at the desks and files, then looked at the clerks, who were bent over their desks. As one of the girls straightened momentarily, he recognized her. He'd seen her earlier, in the snack bar. He looked more closely at her desk. She had reason, he thought for that radiation of uncertain fear he could sense.

"What's in those files?" he demanded.

"It's a complete index to all subscribers, sir."

Kirk looked a little surprised. Morely recognized that the man thought the question a little foolish. He cleared his throat growlingly.

"Let's see one of those cards."

Kirk walked to the file, pulled a small envelope at random, and held it out. The district leader examined it.

"Hah!" he snorted. "I thought so. Duplication of effort. This has nothing on it that isn't in my quarters and locator files."

"There's billing information on the back, sir," Kirk, pointed out. "And current charge slips are kept in the envelope. We use these to prepare the subscriber bills, as well as to maintain the directory service. It's a convenience file, to speed up our work."

Morely turned the envelope over in his hands. "Oh, yes." He opened the envelope, to look at the slips inside. "How do you get the information for these?"

"The charge slips come from Long Lines, sir." Kirk paused. "We get billing information for basic billing from the counters in the dial machine. The other information comes from installation reports and from the quarters file section and the locator files."

MORELY HANDED the envelope back.

"I can see, Kirk," he said, "that you've built up a whole subsection of unnecessary people here." He stepped over to the file cabinets, examined their indices, then pulled a drawer open. He pulled his notebook out, consulted its entries, and searched out an envelope. For a moment, he compared it with the notebook. Then, he turned, holding out the envelope.

He looked at the desks and felt a wave of consternation. Kirk spread his hands.

"But we have the information we need close at hand, sir. Our directory has been coming out on time, and in accurate condition. And our billing is well organized. The directory and billing are my respons—"

Morely waved a hand, then tapped himself on the chest with a long forefinger. "The entire operation of this headquarters is my responsibility, Kirk," he said positively, "and mine alone. And I mean to take care of it. You're responsible to me that Fixed Communications are kept in order, and I don't mean to relieve you of a bit of that responsibility. But I won't have you making jobs and wasting funds on excess personnel." He snorted. "Convenience files are all right. But they're meant to save work, not make it."

Kirk shook his head. "A decentralization will make it difficult," he began.

Again, Morely cut him off. "Don't start telling me why you can't do something," he snapped. "Work out a way you *can* do it. Make up plans for transferring this filing function to Quarters Files, and work up a plan for transferring your billing to Fiscal. That's their business, and they know how to handle it. Submit your study to me this afternoon." He looked around the office again.

"The people in Files and Fiscal can handle this workload without adding a single person. And they will. You're using four clerks to swing it. Kirk, I want this organization to run efficiently, and excess personnel don't lead to economic operation." He stared at the section chief.

"Give these four people their notices today, and I'll expect some suggestions from you as to further streamlining of your section within the next two days. And be sure they're sound suggestions, which result in personnel savings. Otherwise, I'll be looking for a new section chief up here."

For a few seconds, he stood, enjoying the waves of consternation and futile anger which beat about him. Almost, he could pick up some of the despairing thoughts in detail. The clerks, of course, were second-class citizens. And without employment, they'd soon lose their luxury privileges. Unless they were fortunate enough to find other employment very soon, they'd have to move to subsistence quarters, and learn to do without all but the most meagre of food, clothing, and shelter. When they did get employment again, they'd appreciate it. He looked majestically around the office once more, then turned and strode away.

He went through the corridor to the elevator, and stepped in, smiling contentedly. The morning hadn't been entirely wasted.

As he got out of the elevator on executive level, he glanced at his watch. It wasn't quite time for lunch, but there would be little point in spending the few remaining minutes in his office. He walked slowly toward the executive cafeteria.

AFTER LUNCH, he returned to his office. A few matters awaited his examination and decision, and he busied himself for a short time, disposing of them. He paused over the last.

It was a request from Kirk for more cable construction. The justification showed figures which indicated an increase in executive type communications during the past few months. This, coupled with new quarters construction, necessitated additions to the cable trunks from the main exchange. There was added a short survey of necessary repair to existing cable facilities.

Morely leaned back. If he approved the request, he would be helping Kirk increase his section. On the other hand, if he disapproved it, and the communicator lines became congested, he might find himself open to criticism later. Some of his satisfaction evaporated. He looked sourly at the paper.

Suddenly, he thought of Bond's new project. The man had claimed this device could serve as a communication means between its wearers, and had demonstrated that his claim had some truth. After noting the slight fatigue the device seemed to cause in this application, and the vagueness of the device's operation, Morely had disregarded the claim. But junior executives could put up with a little fatigue and inconvenience. And he could see that they did. It might even cut down the time they were always wasting, talking with one another. He rubbed his chin with one hand.

"Well," he told himself, "let's see how it works."

From the way Bond had acted in his office, the sector leader might be still wearing his headband. In fact, he probably was. Morely concentrated on the man, then concentrated on a single, peremptory thought.

"Bond! Can you receive me?"

The answer was prompt. *"Yes, sir. You wanted me?"*

"Of course, Idiot. Why do you think I called? Do you really believe these things would be suitable for routine communication? Could they supplement our normal system?"

"Certainly, sir. They should be very effective."

"Have you offered them to Consolidated yet?"

"Yes, sir. They've accepted them. They're beginning to tool up for production."

Morely winced. He had given the order, to be sure—and before creditable witnesses. Bond had been right in taking immediate action, and his speed would have been commendable in most cases. But this time, Morely regretted his subordinate's efficiency. It was possible the devices might have a practical use after all. Possibly he had been hasty in releasing them to the open market. He shrugged away his thoughts. After all, an administrator had to make quick decisions. He returned to his unusual conversation.

"*Set up a line in research and make up sufficient of those communicators to outfit the executive personnel of this district.*"

"*Yes, sir.*"

"*And give me delivery as soon as you possibly can. How soon will that be?*"

"*We can do it in five days, sir.*"

"*Make it three. That's all.*"

Morely took off his headband. It wasn't as good as a communicator sphere, but it would be good enough. He looked at the request from Communications. Possibly, he would be able to cut Kirk down still more. He scrawled a "disapproved" on the sheet and initialed it. He started to toss the sheet to the corner of his desk, then hesitated.

Drawing the request back to him, he added: "Two subjects on same request. Resubmit as separate requests." He tossed the sheet to the desk corner, for the clerk to pick up. Let Kirk make up new requests, then worry about why his new construction request was still disapproved. He could always be advised to resubmit later, if the headbands didn't work out.

MILES AWAY, Bond turned to an engineer.

"Tool up and start producing these communicators as fast as you can make 'em, Morris. I'll tell you when to stop. The

Old Man just ordered a batch of 'em, and this is one order I want to comply with, and fast!"

He walked toward the small production office. Let's see, he had to produce enough for all the exec personnel in the district. Have to start finding out just how many of those guys there were.

"Make delivery as soon as possible, huh? Cut my estimate by two days? I'll have 'em out over night, if I have to start driving people to do it."

MORELY LOOKED up as the communicator beeped. He reached to the control panel and touched the switch. The face of his deputy appeared in the sphere.

"The section chiefs and field leaders are in the conference room, sir."

"Very good." Morely pushed back his chair. "I'll be right in."

He stepped through the door and crossed the outer office to the conference room. As he entered, there was a rustle of motion. The section chiefs and field leaders stood at attention around the table, waiting. At each place at the table was a blank notepad. The district leader went immediately to the head of the table and sat down.

"Gentlemen," he began, "I'll make this short. I've called you in to try out a new device which I intend to use to help solve the ever-present problem of communication." He looked toward Ward Kirk, who had glanced up in surprise.

"From time to time," he continued, "requests for more and more communicator lines have been coming in to my office. Since no one else seemed to be able to do anything about it, I decided it was time for me to step in. After all, we can't expand our cables indefinitely. We haven't unlimited funds at our disposal and there are other projects demanding attention. Important projects.

"A new electronic development has come to my attention, and it promises to relieve the load on our communicators. Each of you will be issued one of these devices, which I believe are called 'mental communicators,' or something of the sort. And you will draw sufficient of them to outfit those of your people who have occasion to use communication to any large degree. You will use them for all routine communications." He nodded to his deputy, who stepped to the door and beckoned.

Two men came in, carrying cartons, which they distributed around the room. Morely waited until one of the cartons was in the hands of each of the men before him, then he reached up to touch the headband he was wearing.

"This is the device I'm speaking of," he said. "Each of you will wear one of these at all times while you are on duty. You will find, after a little practice, that you will be able to call any associate who is similarly equipped. And you will use them in place of the conventional communications whenever possible." He cleared his throat raspingly.

"Sufficient of these devices have been produced to outfit all the key people of this district. I shall leave it to you to distribute them to your subordinates, and to instruct those subordinates in their use. And I shall expect the load on our communicator cables to be appreciably diminished." He looked to one side of the room.

"Bond."

"Yes, sir."

"You will instruct those present in the use of this new communicator." Morely rose and left the room.

AS THE district leader disappeared through the door, Harold Bond walked to the front of the room. In his hands, he held one of the headbands and a power pack.

"Gentlemen," he said, "this is a form of communicator. I don't pretend to understand precisely how it operates, though I watched its development and set up a production line for it. All I know is that it works. And I know how to use it—to some extent.

"The district leader remarked that one could learn to use it with a little practice, and he's right. Basically, anyone can use it as soon as he puts it on for the first time. But it's like so many other tools. The more you use it, the more proficient you get with it. And I suspect it has capabilities I haven't found yet." He shrugged.

"Operation is simple in the extreme. Since the first model, refinements have been added, and it's unnecessary now for an operator to make any adjustments, other than intensity."

He picked up the power pack.

"This is the power pack, which is plugged into the headband, thus." He paused as he connected the two plugs.

"If you gentlemen will perform the operations as I do, this will take only a short time."

There was a crackling in the room as cartons were opened. Power packs and headbands rattled against the table for a moment, then Bond continued.

"Having plugged in the power pack, you turn this small knob very slightly in a clockwise direction, then place the headband on your head. The knob is the switch and intensity control, and it's quite sensitive. Most people need very little intensity. If you have difficulty with communication, raise the intensity a little at a time, till thoughts come through clearly." He paused, as the men before him adjusted the headbands to their heads.

"The power pack," he continued, "may be placed in a pocket." He reached down. "Personally, I carry mine in my shirt, since I find that convenient."

He looked around the room. Men were turning to stare at their neighbors. Bond could detect a current of uncertainty, then a sensation of pleased surprise. Snatches of thought drifted to him. He ignored them for the moment. Time enough to become acquainted with people later. He placed a hand over his mouth, so everyone could see he was not speaking.

"Can everyone receive me?"

There was a wave of affirmation, and Bond nodded.

"Simple, isn't it? Are there any questions?"

A jumble of thoughts made him waver. Most of them could have been phrased, "How does this thing work? What does it do? Am I dreaming?" Bond smiled in real amusement. He held up a hand.

"I felt the same way," he thought reassuringly. *"Sometimes. I still do. All I can tell you is what you've already found out for yourselves. It works. I'm told it's a sort of telepathic amplifier and radiator. But as I told you, I don't understand its principles. As to practice? I'm still meeting interesting people. So will you."* He took off the headband.

"If anyone has any further questions on operation, I'll try to answer them," he thought quickly. He glanced around the room. Three men were looking at him blankly. He took careful note of them, and mentally shook hands with himself. They were the ones he'd thought would blank out. He spoke aloud.

"I'm sorry, gentlemen," he apologized. "I forgot I might be out of communication. I'm not completely used to this mentacom, myself." He looked toward the deputy leader.

"Do you have anything to add, sir?"

The deputy shook his head. "No," he said thoughtfully. "I think the demonstration was adequate. He cast a quizzical look at Bond, then looked around the room.

"You gentlemen will find a supply of these devices in the outer office. You may draw one for each person you wish outfitted. If any of you have further questions, I would suggest you get in touch with Community Research. They understand this thing." He waved toward the door. "This meeting is adjourned."

He watched as the men filed from the room, then turned on Bond.

"WHAT WAS that business after you took off your headband?" he demanded. "I received you perfectly, and so did practically everyone here. Why the apology?"

Bond grimaced visibly. "We…uh…found out something rather peculiar while we were making the preliminary tests on this device, sir," he explained. "Some people don't seem to be able to pick up clear thoughts with it, unless another person uses the mentacom to drive into them. Most of us can pick up thoughts from anyone we look at, whether they have a band on or not. Definite, surface thoughts, that is."

"And?" The deputy's expression was still questioning. He reached up to point at the band he was still wearing. "I'm getting some mighty peculiar secondary thoughts right now," he added.

"And the people who can't use the device fully have other peculiarities, sir. I'd rather not go into detail. You can find out the whole story for yourself with a very short bit of experimentation, and you have a subject right at hand. If I simply told you, you probably wouldn't believe me anyway."

The deputy nodded slowly. "For the moment," he said, "I'll take your words—and your thoughts—as true. Now, one more question: Can a person, using one of these things, successfully lie to another person who wears one?"

"No, sir." Bond was positive. "It's impossible."

"I got that impression. Thanks." The deputy turned and walked out of the door. Bond looked after him, a slight smile growing on his lips.

"Old Man wanted 'em," he told himself. "He's got 'em."

THE FISCAL chief glanced through the letter in his hands, then canted his head a little and read again. He lowered it to his desk, then sat for a moment, to stare into space. Finally, he looked down once more.

Central Coördination Agency
Office of the Comptroller

CCA 7.338   21 July, 2012

To: District Leader
           District Twelve
           Region Nine
Attn.:   Fiscal Chief
Subject: Mental Communicator

1. It has been brought to the attention of this office that a product known as the "Consolidated Mental Communicator" is being manufactured in District Twelve, Region Nine, and offered for sale as a luxury item.

2. The characteristics of this device have been investigated by the Technical Division, Central Coördination Agency, and it has been found that the device does in fact permit communication between persons by telepathic or some similar means.

3. This device is presently being offered for sale in retail luxury stores throughout the nation. The volume of sales and of potential sales warrants distribution of the manufacturing load to manufacturers other than the Consolidated Electronics Company, who, it is understood, presently hold an exclusive manufacturing agreement with the office of the District Leader, District Twelve, Region Nine. This

arrangement is inconsistent with the sales and use potential of the device in question.

4. The agreement between District Twelve, Region Nine, and the Consolidated Electronics Company will be forwarded immediately to this headquarters for consideration. It is contemplated that this agreement will be terminated and replaced by a manufacturing license from the Products Division, Central Coördinating Agency, who will further license other manufacturers to produce this device.

By Command of Chief Coördinator Gorman

KELLER
Comptroller

MRK/pem

The Fiscal chief shook his head. This one spelled trouble—in capitals. The royalty payments from Consolidated had become one of the major sources of income for the district. And Morely had ordered project after project, using those funds to pay for them. Some of the projects were still outstanding. The Old Man would blow his top.

He looked again at the small scrap of paper which was clipped to the letter. On it was scrawled: "DeVore—See me—HRM."

For a moment, DeVore considered using his own mentacom, then he discarded the idea. To be sure, the leader had insisted that his subordinates use the devices for their own communications, and he'd cut Fixed Communications to the bone. But he still insisted on either communicator calls or personal contact when he wished to talk to any of his people. And he discouraged any but essential use of the communicator system, generally demanding that people come in to see him.

DeVore wrinkled his face disgustedly. It *was* hard to communicate with the district leader by means of a headband. There was a repellent characteristic about the man's mental emanations, and he seemed to fail to comprehend nuances of meaning. Similes, he ignored completely. Thoughts had to be completely and clearly detailed, then phrased into normal, basic wordage before he would acknowledge them. None of the short-cuts used by other members of the administrative staff seemed to work out in his case. He apparently didn't notice visualizations, and he never made one. His transmission was as stiff and labored as the type of communication he required from others—more so, if anything. DeVore scratched his neck.

"How," he asked himself, "does one define a telepathic monotone?"

There were a few others with whom DeVore had experienced similar difficulties, but most people, he had found, picked up meanings and concepts without difficulty— even seemed to anticipate at times. And since the new induction mentacoms had come on the market, with the annoying contacts and headstraps removed, virtually everyone seemed to be either in possession of one of the devices, or about to get one. And, they were worn everywhere.

He smiled as he thought of the young father-to-be, who had bored through the evening traffic rush yesterday. The youngster had been so intent on getting his wife to the hospital that he'd probably failed to see half the ships that clawed out of his way. And his visualization had been almost painfully clear. He'd probably be apologizing for weeks to everyone he contacted.

DeVore straightened in his chair. What would happen, he wondered, if the leader ever ran into one of those situations?

"Yipe!" he muttered. "What a row that would be."

He shrugged, got out of his chair, and walked out into the corridor.

"Better get it over with," he told himself.

AS HE approached the leader's door, it opened, and Ward Kirk came out. He closed the door with a careful gentleness, then faced it for an instant. DeVore was conscious of a wave of hopeless fury, and a fleeting glimpse of Morely's face, framed by brilliant flame. Then, Kirk faced around and saw him.

"*Careful,*" DeVore thought. "*You're broadcasting. He'll pick you up.*"

Kirk grimaced and DeVore saw a faint image of a tyrannosaur, which reared up, jaws agape. Blood dripped from the human figure gripped in the creature's talons.

"*The old...wouldn't understand if he did.*"

DeVore grinned. "*See what you mean. Well, guess I'm the next victim.*"

He stepped to the door and tapped.

"Come in."

Morely looked up as his Fiscal Chief entered, then swept some papers aside. "Well, what do *you* want?"

DeVore held out the letter. "You wanted to see me, sir, about this." He placed the paper within the reach of his superior, who snatched at it, held it up for a moment, then dropped it to his desk.

"Yes, I did. What can we do about it?"

"Why," DeVore spread his hands slightly, "we'll have to comply."

"That isn't what I meant, Idiot! How can we continue to receive the payments from Consolidated?"

"I don't think we can, sir. If Central Coördinating wants to put the device on a national basis, we can't do anything about it."

Morely looked down at the letter, then glared searchingly at DeVore. "The way I read this," he declared, "they want to distribute manufacturing rights on the communicator to plants in other regions than this. Right?"

"Yes, sir."

"But they don't say anything about our continuing the Consolidated payments on an overwrite basis, for the sale of devices they may make. Now, do they?"

"No, sir. But that's implied. In cases like this, Central always takes over all rights." DeVore hesitated. "I believe regulations—"

"I don't care what's implied, DeVore. And I don't care what you believe. All I see is what's in this letter. They want to distribute the manufacturing load, and I'm quite willing that they should. I want to continue receiving the payments from Consolidated. Now, you arrange it so that they're satisfied and I'm satisfied."

"But that'll mean Consolidated will have to pay double. We can't—"

"Don't say 'can't' to me!" Morely held up a hand angrily. "DeVore, I'm not going to tell you how to do this. I want it done. The details are your affair, and if I have to teach you your business, I'll get someone who can do things without having to have them spelled out to him." He leaned back, to glare at DeVore.

"Now, get on the job. I told you to make arrangements for me so that we will retain our payments from Consolidated. And I'm not interested in what arrangements you make with them, or what arrangements they make with Central. Is that a simple enough order for you to understand?"

"Yes, sir. I understand all right. But—"

"Good! I'm glad I managed to get at least one simple idea into your head." The spring in the chair twanged as Morely came forward, to poke his head at DeVore. "Now, get to work on it."

He jerked his head down for a quick look at the letter on his desk, then looked up again.

"And I'll expect a report from you by tonight that you've got the matter taken care of."

DeVore looked at his superior expressionless for a heartbeat. He had been given peculiar orders before, and he'd always managed to work out the problems involved. But this was the ultimate. This one seemed to be just plain illegal. And there was no point in arguing further. There was just the barest chance that there might be some legitimate way out. If he challenged the Old Man on an illegal order, he just might get his ears pinned back. He'd simply have to go back to his office and try to hunt out a technicality. He nodded.

"Yes, sir. I'll get on it immediately."

He saluted and started to leave the office. But he didn't make it.

"And, DeVore!"

The Fiscal chief halted abruptly, and turned.

"Sir?"

"I'm getting tired of the negative thinking you people seem to have fallen into lately. I'm sick of going into every routine detail with you. When you got that letter, you should have immediately worked out a method of retaining the royalties. Then, you could have come in and presented it for my approval. That is the kind of work I want. And that's the kind of work I mean to get in the future. Do you understand?"

Sternly, DeVore suppressed a sarcastic thought. He held his mind and face blank and nodded with a semblance of respect.

"Yes, sir."

"Very well." Morely waved a hand. "Now get something done."

AS DEVORE walked through the corridor, he thought over the situation. Of course, the easy way out would be to force Consolidated to continue the payments in addition to their license fees from Central. That could be done. There were all kinds of methods by which pressure could be brought to bear on any company by the district leader's office. And from Consolidated's point of view, double payments could offer a cheap means of keeping out of difficulties. They would be able to pass most of the cost to the consumer by a slight price increase, justified by a minor modification of the devices.

But they wouldn't be happy about it, and there would come a day when an auditing team from Central would be checking in the district. And that would be the day of days!

DeVore turned in at the door to his own office, crossed the room, and sat down at his desk.

To be sure, he could request a share of the fees from Central, and they'd make an award. But they'd never award more than fifty per cent, and it'd be hard to get that much. That was no good. The Old Man would want the same payments he'd been getting.

Or, he could try to negotiate a new agreement with Consolidated, double the royalties, and then request fifty per cent from Central. He grinned wryly. That would be within legal limits, he was sure, but Central knew the present arrangement, and he knew that they knew. And so would most of the interested manufacturers in other regions. The first-class citizens who owned the plants had their own liaison. They'd all balk. Then, Central would invalidate both old and new agreements and refuse compensation of any kind to district. That would be a suicidal course.

He looked up, thinking of one of the girls out in the legal crew.

"Fiscal regulations, please. And Markowitz on royalties, too."

The girl turned half around, and he could see a faint impression of her view of office details. Then, she went to a book rack. For a few seconds, she glanced over the books, then selected two large volumes.

"Shall I look it up, or do you want the books?"

"I'll take them. Might need quite a bit of research."

Shortly, the girl appeared in his doorway. Quickly, she laid the two volumes on his desk.

DeVore nodded his thanks and opened regulations. Some of the paragraphs were delightfully vague, and could be subject to more than one interpretation. But one paragraph was clear and explicit. And that was the one he was concerned with.

A royalty agreement with, or manufacturing license from Central Coördination definitely abrogated any agreement with, or payment to, any lesser headquarters. Such an agreement or license barred any further negotiation between any lesser headquarters and a manufacturer, relating to the product concerned. Double royalties were prohibited in any case.

He pushed the books aside. There was no need of looking in Markowitz. That regulation paragraph took care of this exact situation, and disposed of it neatly. For an instant, he thought of taking the volume in to the leader's office. Then, he remembered the threatening note in the authoritative voice and the flat, deadly thoughts he had noted as secondary's.

That wouldn't work either. He thought of the undercurrent in Kirk's thoughts. Kirk had been carrying a regulation book, he remembered. He contacted the Fixed Communications chief.

"Don't," he was told. *"I tried it. Know what happened?"*

"Go ahead."

"He got the regional director on the communicator. I've been transferred to Outpost. They seem to need a cable maintenance chief up there. And I was lucky at that. I started to protest, and they nearly had me for insubordination." Abruptly, Kirk cut away.

DEVORE STARED unseeingly across the desk. He'd been at Outpost for a short time once, on an inspection trip, and he still remembered the place. At one time, it had been a well supplied, well organized post. At that time, observational duty had been regarded more highly than now, and the place had been desirable for any single officer, though the married men had objected to being separated from their families by the many miles of frozen waste. But that had changed.

Now, Outpost was the end of the line. The dilapidated surface quarters offered poor protection from the fierce cold. Supply ships were rarely scheduled to the place, and were often held up by storms when they were scheduled. Half rations—even quarter rations—were commonplace. He shook his head. Kirk was in real trouble, and there would be no point in joining him. That would help neither of them.

This, he thought, was a situation. Then, he realized something else. From Morely's point of view, it was a perfectly safe situation, with nothing to lose. The district leader could easily disclaim any responsibility for his Fiscal chief's actions in this matter. After all, he hadn't given any detailed instructions. He had made no direct suggestion of any illegal course. He'd merely consulted his Fiscal expert on a technical matter, and if DeVore had seen fit to use an illegal method of solving a problem, it was DeVore's responsibility alone.

To be sure, Morely had been a little emphatic in his order, but that was simply because he was well aware of his Fiscal chief's disinclination to make exhaustive technical research.

DeVore pursed his lips and looked thoughtfully at the regulation book. He might be able to use the same tactic Morely was following—if he were so inclined. He could issue verbal instructions to the sector leader concerned, and Bond might fail to see the trap. Then, he could report to the leader that the matter was taken care of, indorse the letter back to Central, with the agreement copy, and let Bond turn in funds under one of the "miscellaneous received" accounts. In fact, he realized, that was just about what the district leader expected him to do.

He smiled and shook his head. A few months ago, it was possible he could have done that, but even then, he wouldn't have. And now, with the mental communicators in use, it would be a flat impossibility. The trap would be as obvious to Bond as it had been to him. He leaned back in his chair and tapped his fingertips against each other.

The mentacoms, he knew, were in common use by this time, in virtually every office of district, regional, and national administration, as well as by most citizens. And he'd served under Marko Keller once—known him fairly well, too. He shrugged.

It would be a little irregular for a district Fiscal chief to make direct contact with the Coördination Agency's comptroller, but there was nothing like getting the most expert and authoritative advice available. He relaxed, trying to recreate his memories of the man who was now National Comptroller.

MARKO KELLER strode purposefully into the filing section. He could easily get the data he needed by simply contacting one of the clerks, he knew, but he felt an urgent need for personal activity. That conversation with DeVore, way out in Region Nine, had upset him more than he liked to admit, even to himself.

It wouldn't be so bad if it were an isolated incident. Such things could be taken care of by administrative action, and a single instance would cause little disturbance. But there were too many, happening too often. He pulled a file drawer open, violently.

One of the clerks approached. "Can I help, sir?"

Keller turned to look at him. The man, he noted, was wearing one of the late model inductive headbands that had been sold in such quantities lately. Deluxe model, too. Must have cost him at least two months' pay. Like almost everyone else, he was vitally concerned in this latest affair. Keller frowned. He, himself, he realized, was acting childishly. He would simply be wasting time by trying to do this by himself.

"Yes," he growled. "Get me a brief on a few cases like this one." He made full contact with the man, rapidly summarizing his conversation with DeVore, and including DeVore's short flash of his own conversation with Ward Kirk.

"And get a rundown from personnel. Dig up something on their angle, too. Several representative cases. Get a few people to help you— many as you need. I'm going to take this whole mess in to the Chief tomorrow morning."

PAUL GRAHAM swept into the apartment, seized his wife about the waist and swung her into the air, to set her on top of one of his bookcases.

"They've done it, honey," he shouted.

Elaine kicked her heels in a rapid tattoo against the back of the case.

"Paul Graham, you get me down this instant," she ordered indignantly. "Who's done what?"

Graham stepped back and beat on his chest. "Meet the new production manager, Mentacom Division, Consolidated Electronics."

"Production manager? But, Paul, only first-class citizens can hold supervisory positions."

"Not any more. Didn't you have the communicator on for the news? It all came in."

Elaine shook her head and jumped to the floor. "I've a confession to make, Paul. Ever since they stopped the compulsory notices, I haven't had the thing on at all. It bothered me."

Her husband shook his head in mock dismay. "So now, I'm married to an ignoramus." He spread his hands. "She doesn't know what's going on in the great, big world." He shook a finger at her.

"It all busted this afternoon, darling. While you sat around in your splendid isolation, everything turned upside down."

She looked at him indignantly for an instant, then turned toward the kitchen.

"Paul, if you don't stop raving, I'm going to get my mentacom and pry it out of you," she threatened. "Now, you just settle down. Stop talking in circles and tell me what this is all about."

"Oh, all right. If you insist." Graham sank into a chair, looking like a small boy caught in a prank. "First, there are no more first-class citizens—no second-class citizens—not even third-class citizens. Everyone's a citizen again. Period." He threw his hands up.

"You mean—?"

"That's exactly what I mean. No more restrictions. No more compulsory community work. No more quarters inspections. And no more privileges. We've got rights again!

"If you want a dress, you buy it. You don't worry about whether it suits your station. If I can hold a job, I get it. And I did!" He got out of the chair and strode across the room, to sit on the arm of the divan. "And I can do this, if I want to. If I break this thing down, so help me, George, I'll go out and buy a new one." He bounced up and down a little.

"The administrators are going back to their original jobs. They're responsible for defense, in case of enemy attack, and that's all." He paused. "Of course, until sector and district elections can be held, they'll still take care of some of the community functions—some of them, that is. But the elections'll be set up in a few weeks, and we'll be able to choose our own officials for community government."

He bounced to his feet again, strode around the bookcases, and looked down at his desk. Then, he looked around again.

"Corporations are being set up to take over home construction." He held up a hand. "*Home* construction, I said, not quarters. They're commercializing helicopter manufacture, all kinds of repair work, and a lot of other services. And they're going to restore patent rights. That means plenty to us, darling, believe me."

"BUT, BUT why? What happened?"

Graham turned on her. "Elaine," he cried, "haven't you noticed how many people are wearing mentacoms now, all the time? Haven't you noticed the consideration people have been giving each other for the past weeks? Remember what I told you once? If you fully understand a person, you simply can't kick him around. It's too much like taking slaps at yourself. With the exception of a few empathic cripples, who can't use the mentacom properly anyway, everyone, inside the administrative offices, as well as out, recognized that the bureaucracy was simply unworkable as it stood. So, they changed it. Effective immediately."

Elaine stamped her foot. "You know I haven't been out of this apartment," she cried. "And you know why. I simply couldn't stand the treatment I got. I'd have gotten into serious trouble in minutes. So, I've stayed in. I've done my shopping by communicator, and contented myself right here." She paused.

"But how is the new administration going to be supported? What are people going to do? How are they taking it? It's all so sudden, I should think—"

Graham held up a hand.

"Hey," he protested. "One at a time, please! First—remember taxes? Remember how we used to growl about them? They're back. And I love 'em. Second—nobody is going to do anything. Anything drastic or unusual, that is. And finally? Everyone I've seen is taking it in their stride. Seems as though they've been sort of expecting it, ever since they started mind-to-mind communication.

"You'd be surprised how good most people are at it, now that they're used to it. You start into a line of helicopters. All at once, you realize that the guy coming is really in a hurry. He's got to get somewhere, fast. So, you let him go by. The next fellow's not going to be in any tearing rush. He'll let you in, and cheer you on your way.

"You feel like being left alone? Nobody'll even notice you. But if you feel like talking, half a dozen total strangers'll find something in common with you. And they'll discuss it. Honey, you'll be surprised how much you've missed. Get your mentacom. Let's take a little shopping trip."

"And here's one of our more difficult cases. But he's coming along nicely." Dr. Moran pointed through the one-way window.

"Name's Howard Morely. He used to be a district leader, under the bureaucracy. But along in the last few weeks, just before the change, he got into some sort of scrape. They questioned him, and declared him unfit for service. Put him out on a pension." He pulled at an ear.

"Matter of fact, I understand his case had quite a deal to do with the change—sort of triggered it. They tell me it sort of pointed up the fallacies of the bureaucracy." He shrugged.

"But that's unimportant now, I guess. He almost receded into complete paranoia. Had a virtually complete case of empathic paralysis when he came to us. Simply no conception of any other person's point of view, and a hatred of people that was fantastic. But he's nearly normal now."

The visiting psychiatrist nodded. "I've seen the type, of course. We have a number of them, too. You say this new technique was successfully used in his case?"

"Yes. We had doubts of it, too. Seemed too simple. Sure, we're all familiar with the mentacoms by now. Wouldn't be without my own. But the idea of a field generator so powerful as to force clear impressions into a crippled mind like his, without completely destroying that mind, seemed a little fantastic." He shrugged.

"In this case, though, it was a last resort, so we tried it. He resisted the field for days. Simply sat in his cell and stared at the walls. We were almost ready to give up when one of the operators finally got through to him. Know what his first visualization was?"

The visitor shook his head and laughed. "I could try a guess, I suppose," he said, "but my chances would be something less than one in a thousand million."

Moran grinned. "You're so right. There was a whole bunch of kids standing around. Looked like dozens of 'em. And they were all chanting at the top of their voices. You know that old jingle? 'Howie's got a gir-rul?' Chanted it over and over." The grin widened. "Operator said his face stung for ten minutes. That girl must have packed one sweet wallop!"

THE END

If you've enjoyed this book, you will not want to miss these terrific titles…

ARMCHAIR SCI-FI & HORROR DOUBLE NOVELS, $12.95 each

D-51   **A GOD NAMED SMITH** by Henry Slesar
         WORLDS OF THE IMPERIUM by Keith Laumer

D-52   **CRAIG'S BOOK** by Don Wilcox
         EDGE OF THE KNIFE by H. Beam Piper

D-53   **THE SHINING CITY** by Rena M. Vale
         THE RED PLANET by Russ Winterbotham

D-54   **THE MAN WHO LIVED TWICE** by Rog Phillips
         VALLEY OF THE CROEN by Lee Tarbell

D-55   **OPERATION DISASTER** by Milton Lesser
         LAND OF THE DAMNED by Berkeley Livingston

D-56   **CAPTIVE OF THE CENTAURIANESS** by Poul Anderson
         A PRINCESS OF MARS by Edgar Rice Burroughs

D-57   **THE NON-STATISTICAL MAN** by Raymond F. Jones
         MISSION FROM MARS by Rick Conroy

D-58   **INTRUDERS FROM THE STARS** by Ross Rocklynne
         FLIGHT OF THE STARLING by Chester S. Geier

D-59   **COSMIC SABOTEUR** by Frank M. Robinson
         LOOK TO THE STARS by Willard Hawkins

D-60   **THE MOON IS HELL!** by John W. Campbell, Jr.
         THE GREEN WORLD by Hal Clement

ARMCHAIR SCIENCE FICTION CLASSICS, $12.95 each

C-16   **THE SHAVER MYSTERY, Book Three**
         by Richard S. Shaver

C-17   **THE PLANET STRAPPERS**
         by Raymond Z. Gallun

C-18   **THE FOURTH "R"**
         by George O. Smith

ARMCHAIR SCIENCE FICTION & HORROR GEMS SERIES, $12.95 each

G-5   **SCIENCE FICTION GEMS, Vol. Three**
         C. M. Kornbluth and others

G-6   **HORROR GEMS, Vol. Three**
         August Derleth and others